Doves and Angels

Elizabeth Moult

PublishAmerica
Baltimore

First printing

All characters appearing in this work are fictitious. Any resemblance to real persons, living or dead, is purely coincidental.

ISBN: 1-4241-5382-4
PUBLISHED BY PUBLISHAMERICA, LLLP
www.publishamerica.com
Baltimore

Printed in the United States of America

Prelude

November 30, 1995

Peace talks between Bosnia and Herzegovina, the contact group and a European special negotiator produced a signed document called the Dayton Peace Agreement, a promise to bring peace to the troubled area. It included things such as, respect for one another, settling of disputes peacefully, neighborly recognition for one another, mutual bonds, respect for human rights of all, including refugees and displaced persons. Everyone agreed fully with all entities used to implement peace and order. The cease fire agreement of October 5, 1995 continues. Foreign combat forces withdraw behind a zone of separation. All weapons are put away. Bosnia invited a multi-international military implementation force to maintain the peace. People being charged with war crimes are not allowed to participate. All information regarding land mines and arsenal is to be reported. Red Cross sets a plan to release all combatants and civilians.

The annexes of the agreement call for regional stabilization, inter-entity boundary, free elections, constitution, arbitration, powerful human rights, refugee's safe return home, preserved national monuments, shared services, civilian participation, international police task force, everyone agreeing and consenting to abide by the rules.

The Dayton Peace Accord hoped to bring peace and stability. Problem was, they didn't include Kosovo's President Rugova on the agenda. The Albanians in Kosovo wanted an independent state, free from Serbian control. Another problem was that it wasn't signed by the general population, only the politicians. How can you buy into something when you don't read the rules? Peace has to start in the heart of the individual.

January 1999
Small village in Kosovo
"They're coming, they're coming!" Marcia screamed at her family.

"Who is coming?" Alexis, the youngest child asked.

"The rebels. They are going to kill us!" the young mother screamed, terror evident in her voice.

"Why Mommy? Why do they want to kill us?"

"Because we are of a different religion."

Alexis didn't understand. At the tender age of five, she probably would never understand.

"Quick, go in there!" her mother yelled and pointed to the cupboard under the kitchen sink.

That was the last Alexis saw of her family. The last vision was the terrified, anguished look in her mother's eyes.

She had only been in the cupboard for a few minutes when the explosion hit the other end of the house. The cupboard she was in flew a few feet in the air and crashed. Alexis had banged her head. Her leg hurt.

She prayed, "Dear God, please help me. Please." Over and over she prayed, terrified to leave the cupboard and look out.

After a few minutes, she heard a voice, "Alexis, you will be okay. God has sent me to keep on eye on you."

The terrified little girl opened the cupboard to see who was talking. The missile had basically flattened her house. She saw only rubble and dead bodies.

"Who are you?" she asked the voice.

"I am your guardian angel."

April 1999

Nick loaded a new roll of film into his camera, shut the cap and the automatic roller clicked into action. He'd been working on finding lawyers who could tell him all about anti-trust laws. He was sick of the corporate world and wanted to get out and get his hands dirty. He flicked on the TV. His favorite documentary, 'The Compassionate Ear,' was on, staring Margaret, the cute, dark skinned reporter with the French accent. He'd always wondered what her native land was.

She was explaining how a Senior NATO diplomat described Milosevic as the engineer of all wars of post Yugoslavia. He was clever and crueler than anyone expected. The war was simply becoming the ruthless reduction of Kosovo. A mass expulsion of killings, burnt villages, obliteration of people's identity. The NATO bombing campaign was now at a standstill. Nothing was working. While the bombs fell, Milosevic's army continued to push tens of thousands of Albanian Kosovars out of the country, an exodus of dazed, weeping, refugees fleeing along train tracks to avoid land mines, escaping for their lives into the poorest states. Everyone with a horror story to tell.

His army then launched a murderous offensive against the rebel Kosovo Liberation Army, a small militant group who began killing Serb policemen and others who collaborated with the Serbs.

The air powers were futile against the primitive "ethnic cleansing," with guns and knives. The bombing campaign failed to deter the rape of Kosovo women, and even appeared to be increasing it. Because they didn't take out Milosevic, nothing changed. The air strikes did nothing. The bombs fell, the refugees continued to flee and Milosevic refused to budge.

After a week of air raids, people were still being ordered out of their homes at gunpoint. Thousands were marched and packed into trains and all their identification destroyed.

NATO now wondered how to achieve victory. Everyone tossed around several ideas. The White House said they would need

200,000 ground troops. Memories of Vietnam and Somalia haunt them. The Americans say no. NATO won't go without them. Besides, the roads were all covered in land mines, bridges were rigged to explode and they might not arrive in time to stop the exodus from the region.

Back in March, failure of diplomacy with Milosevic paved the way for the largest NATO military action in their fifty-year history. They tried to go back to the table with Milosevic, but no one trusted him. In the end, they decided to continue with the bombs and hope Milosevic buckled.

Nick watched the host of the show.

She spoke with such compassion.

Compassion is a main characteristic of a true humanitarian. According to a psychologist, it was the one thing that had been lacking with everyone in Hitler's regime. She had a cute smile, was incredibly poised, graceful and had a magnetic spirit. He wondered if she was single. She inspired him to report on Kosovo and he wondered if his boss would let him go.

Chapter One

September 1999

Nick ran through the dense bush, tripped on a log, and crashed onto the hard ground. His backpack landed with a thud. He looked around to see if he was being followed and realized he was clutching his camera securely against his chest like one would protect a small infant. He chuckled at his devotion to the story – in the face of fear and at the most dangerous hour of his life he'd protected a photojournalist's most valuable possession—his camera.

Trembling, he pulled off his pack, squirmed into the tall grass and surveyed his surroundings. He thanked God no one had followed him and that he hadn't tripped on a land mine.

The cold wind bit at his nose. He ached for the sun to replace the dark dismal sky that had persisted over Kosovo for almost the entire two weeks he'd been there. He was alone and without the caravan that photojournalists often take with them into danger zones.

The war was pushing everyone into a state of lunacy. Kids were screaming in the streets. There were knives, slaughters, guns and dead bodies. Visions of it all flashed in his mind. He desperately tried to push the thoughts aside, but they persistently returned.

He'd just witnessed carnage, and when he fled, people had been chasing him. He'd outrun them. They would have known he was a Canadian reporter because of the flag on the back of his pack. They would know he would have access to an international media and because of that they might wish him dead. He wasn't stupid—he knew that.

It was a war that was happening because people thought that people of another religion didn't deserve to live and needed to be massacred. He'd been sent to cover the war and report back to the magazine he worked for. But something in his soul was insisting he couldn't report it that way; it simply wouldn't work. He needed something more. Yet he knew that as soon as he returned home, the first thing Jack, his boss, was going to ask for was his article on the war. He would expect him to have it analyzed and dissected like a science experiment. He'd want it written in fancy journalism. It was bullshit. It was people killing each other because they were of a different religion. Ethnic groups who hated each other.

He wondered if everyone worshipped and prayed to the same God. If we did, then why would they fight over religion because religion is God? It didn't make sense.

Then there were the Israelis and Palestine's fighting over the Holy Land. "The rich must help the poor, and so must I." He hummed a song that his uncle used to sing. It was hate. It was about hate. There was no religion to it. If they didn't hate, it wouldn't happen.

Off in the distance, a bird made a screeching noise, making him jump. Suddenly he was jittery. Once again he nervously scanned his perimeter, constantly on guard, fearing someone may jump him any minute.

He recalled history lessons and what most wars had been about. There certainly had been enough of them. People fight over land, oil, and religion. There was always a reason for a war, but the bottom line was if people didn't hate each other, they wouldn't do it. What bred that degree of hate to make people want to kill so violently? Love and peace were special ingredients in the mystics of life. Words that he, as a small child growing up in Canada, had taken for granted.

He was disappointed when he'd heard the Canadians were going to drop bombs in Kosovo. It was like spanking a child for hitting. But the slaughter had gone on long enough. Until peace could be achieved, it was the only language anyone seemed to understand.

This had been the third war in Yugoslavia in less than a century. The latest one in Kosovo already killed close to ten-thousand people. Diplomatic talks with Milosevic had failed. So, on the dawn of the twenty-first century, Canada, one of the international peacemakers, came in as 20% of the NATO air response team. The world needed peace. Hostility breeds hostility, but the bombs had worked before. They crippled Hitler and the Japanese by using them. They calmed down Saddam, the idiot in Iraq, by using them. The world had seen way too much hatred.

He surveyed his surroundings one more time, ensuring no one was around. He bravely pulled himself onto a rock. Tiny birds chirped and it was the most beautiful sound he'd ever heard. They weren't the notorious black birds of Kosovo that were everywhere and nicknamed Alfred Hitchcock's birds from his movie *The Birds*, a horror story. These were tiny, chirpy, birds that made a joyful noise. The sound made him happy. He needed to concentrate on simple happy moments because if he didn't, he would surely go insane.

He shivered in the damp as he ran a hand through his curly black hair, feeling its grease and grime. He thought about Samantha, his sometimes friend, sometimes lover, and longed to be in her oversized tub. There she would rub his back and massage his feet. He visualized the warmth, the flicker of the candles, the sweet aroma of the bath oil and the amazing sex.

Thinking about Samantha and how much she loved him was probably going to be the one thing that would help him stay sane tonight. It was going to be a long night; he could feel it in his bones.

He heard planes and looked into the sky. He could see them, but he wasn't sure who they were. He prayed that help be on the way. Help for all the innocent victims of war and maybe help for him. He desperately wanted to go home. He'd seen enough, taken enough pictures and talked into the tape player over and over again. He'd interviewed enough suffering people.

He hummed the words from Rod Stewart's popular song "Forever Young" *May the Good Lord be with you through every*

ELIZABETH MOULT

road you take. May sunshine and happiness be with you when you are far from home.

He pulled out his cigarette package and counted his smokes. He had five. He didn't care if he ran out of food or water because he could eat birds and drink from the creeks, but whatever happened, he would certainly go insane if he ran out of smokes.

He pushed the thoughts of what he'd just witnessed into the back of his mind. It was sick, grotesque, revolting, and criminally insane. A total Hell on earth. Why were there so many madmen in the world? How could their leaders allow such atrocities to occur? Religion. Is there really a God? He knew there was because God had spoken to him in his kitchen one night. He'd prayed, asking for help winning a lottery. God had paid him a visit. The visitor was exactly as the guy in the movie 'Oh God,' staring George Burns. But Nick didn't believe the voice was genuine, so God told him he was an angel.

God had been upset with him for asking for help with selfish things. Nick asked him why he was wasting his time on him when there was so much suffering going on in the world. God told him he was right.

Nick then spent years trying to figure God out. The way he had it conceived was that he was a manager that sent angels to keep an eye on people or do special missions. Spirits were dead people waiting for another host. Angels were messengers of God.

He wondered about Church and all the formal ceremonies that occur all over the world every Sunday worshipping God because he'd had a conversation in his kitchen with the guy like it was a friendly chat with a neighbor. But he liked the church stuff. He didn't go often, but he liked the music and the candles. He'd watched it on TV a few times and he would go again someday. He figured God probably loves it when people sing and pray to him in a joyous celebration.

Many thoughts were speeding through his mind: the war, work, Samantha, and life in general. He'd been in a mid-life crisis for some time. Now it was over and he was ready to move on with the other half of his life. He started thinking about all of life's philosophies.

You live, you collect things, you go places, you do things, and then you die. Now he sat, all alone, in a war he had nothing to do with.

He wondered if Samantha had grown tired of waiting for him to sew his wild oats and found a new man. He wouldn't blame her if she had. He loved her, but he loved his freedom more. He knew he'd hurt her by sleeping with someone else. He didn't know why he did it. He'd had his share of women in his life, but Samantha was different. She really adored him. But he refused to believe that someone so nice, caring, gentle, sensual, and intelligent could love someone like him but he wasn't going to try and analyze that too.

Everyone warned him how dangerous Kosovo would be. He'd been given the option to back out at any time. He figured he was becoming an adrenaline junkie, thriving off insanity. Now he prayed he got out alive.

The sun was high in the sky. It would be a while before it set. The cold and dampness caused him to shiver. He craved a fire, but that would reveal his location to the rebels.

He searched for inner strength; strength that would help him makes it through the night.

He stared at the ground, lit a cigarette, inhaled it deeply, and watched a squirrel pass. He couldn't stop shaking and trembling. He constantly pushed thoughts about what he'd witness into his unconsciousness. He thought about Samantha and how her love had given him ambition. She'd lit a romantic spark deep inside that had burnt out years ago.

Trees swayed in the wind. He wondered how long he was going to be able to sit on the rock. He needed to move. He didn't want to move. He was getting a hemorrhoid but he didn't care. He wasn't sure how long he'd been sitting, but it must have been a while.

Looking up into the sky, he wished for a chopper to rescue him. His phone was dead. Useless thing.

He glanced over at his heavy pack, the one with the tape recorder and laptop and he considered himself lucky to still have it.

He didn't have much food, a little bottle of water, a stale Rice Krispie square, an apple, bag of chips, three beef jerkys, two kaiser buns and some cheese. It was simply luck that he'd purchased everything before the slaughter happened.

He wanted to leave the pack, just take the food and run, but it was his career, his livelihood. He needed the pay cheque to pay the mortgage on the house he was never at. The house that was falling down because he never did anything to it. It didn't matter. Nothing mattered anymore. Despite everything, he would manage to be happy because that was what life was all about—being happy. He could be happy, anyone can, you just have to tell yourself to do it.

The cold wind was cutting into him. He lit the cigarette again. His lighter was getting low. He reached into his pack and grabbed a can of lighter fluid, shook it and recognized the weight. He had enough for one more refill. "Whew." He wiped his brow, relaxed, took another deep drag, and watched it burn. Staring at the red ember, he watched the smoke. It was going to be a long night.

Clicking into reality, he took one more puff and put it out. Almost a whole cigarette gone, now he only had four. He carefully shoved it into his shirt pocket. Right now they were his most guarded, most valuable possession. When things got so low that low was as low as low could go, he would still have his smokes. They would keep him from reaching the depths of despair. The place where you lose touch with reality and strange things happen to you. His smokes would prevent him from reaching that point.

Now he was really cold and still wanted to light a fire. He was scared. Big, strong Nick was scared. He told himself that he would be okay. He would fight it. He would be brave. Everything would be all right.

He should think happy, positive, love-filled thoughts. Samantha was a happy, positive, love-filled thought. A bit of a pest, but she made him happy. She was a sexually exciting woman. No, he didn't want to think of Samantha because that would make him lonely. He should think about golfing. He would think about golfing because that would make the awful memory go away. It had been an awful sight, an awful thing to witness. He shouldn't think about it.

He looked at his knapsack again and thought about hiding it in the bush but then he would have to return for it. He would have to lug it around and it looked as though it weighed the same as a bulldozer. He decided to leave it for now. He was sure he would never be able to golf ever again. Where would he get the energy to do something like that? Golf was now memories but at least he had them. He recognized he must be in shock or something. Who wouldn't be after what he'd just witnessed?

He was in some kind of a posttraumatic stress situation and had every right to be. When the sun set he would probably have the nervous break down he deserved. He hoped it didn't get too cold. He wanted to collect wood. The sun was getting lower in the sky and he was getting hungry. A nice hot meal would be good. Samantha loved candlelight dinner with good food, good wine, and fun conversation. He wanted that again.

Ethnic cleansing. Fucking ethnic bullshit was more like it. It was such a senseless, pointless thing. He tried to figure it out, the reason behind it. There was so much history behind some of it, but basically it was hate. He thought about the famous figure skating star and native Russian, Katarina Whit who had skated in dedication to the women of Sariajova at the Olympics. She'd asked the world for peace. It had been a beautiful skate, full of emotion. But even it hadn't stopped bullshit. Hadn't anyone seen her skate? It was a powerful message she tried to send to the world, but it too was ignored.

He felt proud that the Canadians had played host to almost thirty-thousand refugees, providing them with temporary shelter. A refugee is someone who is fleeing danger. It is a person who flees to a foreign country or power to escape danger or persecution. The refugees were grateful. The majority of Canadians welcomed them with open arms, proud to be able to help.

And now, as he sat here, surrounded by the horror of it, he wanted to invite them all back home with him when he left. Most had lost everything: their homes, their businesses, entire villages of people slaughtered. Stop it. Stop it. He had to stop thinking about it. He would go crazy if he didn't stop.

At one point they trained the Canadian peacekeepers to kill on the spot anyone caught slaughtering. One peacekeeper he'd interviewed gave him a cold, icy stare and told him it was his job. It was what he was trained to do. He hoped his smile would protect him from harm. A smile. The peacekeeper was counting on his smile to protect him from harm. Wow, it was too much, but the kid did have a nice smile.

The sun was behind a cloud. There was still about five hours of daylight left.

He rummaged around in the bottom of his pack until he found his bottle of whisky safely wrapped in his rugby coat. He sipped it slowly, felling it burn going down. Now he was hungry and cold, but the little bit of whisky helped him mentally.

He was sad, lonely and wanted to cry. He was writing about gruesome stuff so the magazine he worked for could publish it for the entire world to see. Would it help? That was the ultimate goal, to get the message out so someone would stop it. The world needed to know, but more importantly, the world had to know. It was a had-to-know kind of thing.

What was with the birds? The sun was slowly reaching the horizon. Soon it would be dark. Then what? He pulled his penlight from his pocket and tested it. It barely worked. He couldn't remember if he had a spare battery. He hoped he did. He should check before it got dark. Ah, screw it. He thought about getting out his tape recorder and taping his feelings just in case he wanted to do a piece about what it was like to sit in the bush too scared to move. Ah, screw that too. He could see lights off in the distance. They looked to be many miles away.

How he missed Samantha.

He took another sip of whisky and watched the sun set behind a field. He took another sip and relaxed a bit more. He wanted to help stop the insanity, but how? Maybe he should ask God for help. Yes, he would try that. "God, this is me, the one with the lottery, only this time it's something really different. I need your help. I need you right now to please come and help me do something to help the world peace problem."

He sat and waited for an answer but no response. He watched the sun set and the sky turned pretty colors. The wind died.

After a few minutes he decided he needed to be more formal. He should be praying to God in a more formal manner. He needed a candle. Yes, that would do it.

He found a small candle that he'd picked up off the road several days ago, lit it, and stood up. It felt good to stretch after sitting on a rock for so long.

He knelt down beside the candle, folded his hands and bowed before the God he knew.

"Dear Father in Heaven, I ask you, I pray to you and I beg you to help me find a way to end this insanity. There must be a way. Please God, help me find the way." He dropped his head into his arms and rested. Suddenly a large gust of wind appeared and blew out the candle. He sat and stared at it, wondering if it was a sign. Had God sent him a sign?

Night came and as expected it was extremely dark. The blackness created an obscurity of gloom. He was sure he was losing his mind, he could feel it happening. But he would survive because he was strong. He was a fighter. One who never quits. One who always relied on his smokes to calm him down. He still had four.

He doesn't remember how long he lay with his head resting on the rock but it must have been a while. The wind was wiping from all directions. He continued to shiver.

He should eat something before his blood sugar level dropped too low.

He sat up and looked around. He heard a little voice. "It's the politicians," the voice told him. "You need to deal with the politicians, the United Nations and the International Charter of Human Rights." It was a faint voice. He barely heard it.

"What? Tell me more."

There was no response.

The Politicians? That was his clue? He needed to deal with the politicians? He needed to get out of the woods alive. Before that he needed to make it through the night. He grabbed a kaiser bun, ate it quickly, hoping the carbohydrates would keep him warm.

He thought about the voice. It had been a feminine voice, so it wasn't God. He wondered whom? And now he had to figure out what to do with the information. It was Serbian President Slobodan Milosevic who was responsible for the current destruction. It was Milosevic who was not threatened by the air strikes and it was Milosevic who continued to allow the insanity to continue. It was Milosevic who responded to the bombings by sending out death squads and herding tens of thousands of Kosovar Albanians on to buses and trains, and driving them across the mountainous border into neighboring Balkan countries. No problem. He would just march right into Milosevic's office and tell him to quit. That should do it. He would listen to him because he was Nick. Samantha once told him that she would love him forever. He'd taken the information and turned it into a source of strength. He must remember to thank her when he returned home. If she would talk to him ever again.

He thought about what a wonderful country he lived in, how proud he was of his heritage and the fact that numerous ethnic, cultural and religious groups happily and peacefully live under one sane government.

Canada is one of the strongest, vibrant and diverse democratic societies on the globe. Its core values of freedom, democracy, rule of law and human rights make it a leader on the worlds stage. It's a country where people from around the globe have come to make a home and form one of the most peaceful, multi-cultural and free societies ever known to mankind.

He knows that many of Canada's ancestors carved this amazing civilization from the scruff of the land and that with their hard work, determination, and dedication, created this amazing country.

When our freedom, and the freedom of our friends was threatened, many answered the call of duty to wipe out tyranny so that we could continue to enjoy a life of freedom and dignity.

Canada is a role model to the world and is poised to enter the twenty-first century in the limelight on the global stage of freedom and fairness.

Nick is proud to be a Canadian.

He needed a fire. He felt around for wood, but it was too dark. He gazed at the candle for the longest time, sitting there, staring, and thinking. Thinking about politicians. How? How was he was going to get through to them to change their way of thinking? To make positive change that would end the bullshit? He racked his brain over and over, trying to figure it out. It had been going on for decades. Decades, now that was a joke. He was sure the fighting had been going on since cave man days. He hadn't known that much about Kosovo when he first received the assignment, so he went on a fact-finding mission in his Encarta disc. It had taken forever to find information on Kosovo. He first thought it was in Russia. It's not. It's a province of Yugoslavia on the land mass known as Europe and is part of the Balkan Peninsula, which includes the countries of Slovenia, Croatia, Bosnia, Herzegovina, the Former Yugoslav Republic of Macedonia, Serbia, Montenegro, Albania, Greece, Romanis, Bulgaria and European Turkey. He had to look under regions of the world to find the Balkan Peninsula and he'd found a lot of information about it. Serbia is the Northern Province to Kosovo and a republic of Yugoslavia. Since prehistoric to modern time, the area has been occupied by numerous people and nations and it is the most screwed up place politically. The fighting had been going on as far back as the year 44 AD when the Romans conquered it. One time Serbia was part of the ancient country of Illyria. The Balklans once were Roman provinces. The peninsula remained part of the Byzantine Empire until the late Middle Ages when Ottoman Turks invaded and gradually took control of almost the entire peninsula.

Who cared what all the wars were about? What was important now was that it needed to stop. The visions of the horror he'd witnessed kept popping in and out of his mind. He pushed them aside, constantly hoping they would never return.

There has rarely ever been true peace in Kosovo. Currently, the population is two-million, 90% Ethnic Albanians and 7% Serbs. The Croats are in there some place too.

Several significant dates include 1389 when the Ottoman Turks defeated the Serbs. The fighting continued and in 1459 Serbia ended up under Turkish rule. In 1828, following the Russo-Turkish war, Serbia gained greater autonomy and the number of Turkish garrisons were reduced.

The nineteenth century brought about the emergence of political identity, military and political strife. During that time, one Balkan nation after another won independence from the Turks. The various small Balkan countries emerged from the revolt against Turkish rule as autonomous nations.

After World War I ended in 1918, Bosnia, Herzegovina, the Provinces of Croatia, Slavonia and Carniola united with Serbia and Montenegro to become the Kingdom of the Serbs, Croats and Slovenes, later named Yugoslavia.

In 1929, the leaders of Serbia, Coatia, and Montenegro proclaimed the kingdom of the Serbs, Croats, and Slovenes, which became the kingdom of Yugoslavia.

And, of course, Hitler had stuck his nose in. During World War II in 1941, Germany invaded Serbia and established a puppet state. Yugoslavia and Greece fell to the Germans early in 1941 despite stubborn resistance, but eventually ended up as the kingdom of Greece and the Republic of Yugoslavia. Between the two world wars, statesmen tried to prevent the Balklan countries from again becoming the "powder keg" of Europe.

In 1974, Serbian politician Slobodan Milosevic rose to power and curtailed public funding for Albanians.

In 1981, the Albanian majority sought independence, but changes made in the Serbian Constitution and abolishment of the Parliament and Government of Kosovo prevented it. Since then, Serbian authorities have continued on a policy of repression, rape and murder against Albanians as they try to become independent.

A contact group consisting of the United States, United Kingdom, Germany, France, Italy and Russia, met to try and establish a policy for peace and issued four demands: cessation of fighting, withdraw of Serb forces, return of refugees and unlimited access for international monitoring.

In 1991,Yugoslavia began to splinter. Serbia sought to hold the republics together, trying to maintain its dominant position and to protect the Ethnic Serb minorities in the other republics. Croatia, Slovenia, and Bosnia-Herzegovina declare independence from Yugoslavia, triggering ethnic fighting between Croats, Muslims, and Serbs. A year later, total war broke out in Bosnia.

In April of 1992, four of the six constituent republics of Yugoslavia declared their independence (Slovenia, Croatia, Bosnia, and Herzegovina) and the remaining two (Serbia and Montenegro) united and declared themselves the new Yugoslavia. But the international community refused to recognize the name and would not allow it in the United Nations.

The Clinton administration and the contact group tried to negotiate with Milosevic to remove Special Forces and establish an acceptable future status of Kosovo.

NATO studied a variety of options for dealing with them, and in 1992, President Bush warned Milosevic that the United States was prepared to use military force against Serb-instigated attacks in Kosovo.

By 1994 the intense fighting between ethnic Serbs and Albanians continued.

The Dayton Peace agreement was signed in November of 1995 by the leaders of Bosnia, Croatia and Serbia. Everyone agrees to implement peace and order. While peace talks were occurring in Paris, Milosevic continued with ethnic cleansing and broken peace promises.

They neglected to include Kosovo's President Rugova in the talks. The Albanians in Kosovo wanted to be free from control of Milosovic. Violence continued.

On March 31, 1998, the United Nations Security Council condemned the excessive use of force by Serbian police against civilians. Through the arms embargo on Yugoslavia and Chapter Seven of the United Nations Charter, they determined the violence in Kosovo was a threat to international peace and security. They tried everything. Unarmed peacekeepers, armed peacekeepers, combs, the Canadian Aces, moved refugees out of harm's way and still there was fighting.

By late September 1998, NATO issued an activation alert that military action was possible. In October of 1998, NATO allies authorized air strikes against Serb military targets. Milosevic agreed to withdraw troops, but between January and March of 1999, Serb police continue their attacks.

On March 24th 1999, NATO forces began air operations over the Federal Republic of Yugoslavia.

By November of 1999, Serbian Special Forces continued attacks and drove almost 800,000 Kosovo Albanians from their homes into forest and mountains. With the Balklan winter approaching, this created an impending humanitarian disaster. A second wave of air strikes began.

The main language is Serbo-Croatian, which he would never be able to learn, so he doesn't even try.

Growing up in Canada as a small child, he never understood war. He knew Poppy Day was something very important. It had to be because they always went to the auditorium and someone in a uniform would play the bugle. They would have to sit quietly for two minutes, hoping their friends wouldn't tickle them and get everyone into trouble.

A bird shrilled, which caused him to jump. Every bone moved. It felt like an electric current was running battery acid through his veins. He heard the shrill again and looked around to see where the noise came from. In his spellbound stupor he spied a buzzard. Hawk and buzzard, same thing. He knew because he'd studied them and written about them once when they had been on the endangered species list. There used to be a lot of them along the North Atlantic coast, but they reduced in numbers when DDT and other pesticide residues in the food interfered with reproduction. But with the banning of these chemicals, they have made a remarkable recovery.

He wanted a happy ending for Kosovo. He wanted to write that the fighting had stopped once and for all.

He thought about his ancestral Ireland, another place where they fight about everything and anything. If you ask what the fighting is about most people will give you a different story: land, money or religion.

He tracked the buzzard to the tree and could see the big nest nest high in the branches; a place they return to each year from winter migration. Some actually breed in the same nest year after year.

He heard more shrilling whistle cries. It sent shivers down his spine. There were several of the beautiful birds, but their shrill cries made him cringe. Between them and the blackbirds, he was getting his dose of sky creatures.

He grabbed his whisky and took a large gulp. It took away the edge. He was still thinking about how to stop the fighting.

The temperature continued to drop. He was really shivering. He found a warm sweater and put it on under his coat. He loved the woods and knew some survival techniques. He wasn't afraid of the woods, it was the fighting he was afraid of. He didn't want to die tonight in this Hell on earth. It was cold, dark and there were buzzards in the sky. Heck, who wouldn't be freaking under those conditions?

He could envision Samantha gazing at him. He thought about how much she enjoyed making love. She was a great lover. He quickly got a boner, but it dissipated.

He decided he needed to pray again for more help with the political thing because he didn't quite understand the message. He lit the candle and kneeled in prayer. "Oh God, where are you?"

One of the hawks shrieked.

He jumped. "Dear God, please, I need more help. I don't know how to deal with the politicians. What do I do with them?"

He waited for a voice, a sign, anything that would guide him. He stared into the glow of the candle and felt its mesmerizing sensation.

He loved fire. Again he visualized Samantha, draped in her long evening gown, blond hair bouncing off her shoulders and lighting candles. She'd have a horny look on her face and seduce him like no other.

He checked his watch. It was almost midnight. The night was young.

He thought about the star filled sky at home and how much he loved to watch Samantha dance under the starry sky and full moon. Oh how she loved to dance under the moon. He could see her floating in the skylight…floating…. floating…. The hawks screeched again. Mentally he didn't know how much more he was going to be able to take.

The night dragged on; the long, dark, cold, lonely night. The dampness was in every bone and muscle. He hoped a pack of wild dogs didn't attack him. The buzzards screeched again and again.

He wondered how many people had been on this rock before him. Probably zillions. People have inhabited this end of the earth for thousands of years. Almost every forest had been replanted from being something else at one time. He hoped he wasn't on an Indian burial ground.

His nerve ending fried like the heat of a hot iron His candle melted to a tiny flicker and he had no other. The tiny flame melted away.

Then it happened. The tiny flick-of-flame extinguished. He heard the voice again. "At dawn the angels will sing and the doves will fly."

The buzzards screeched.

What was that tiny noise? He repeated it in his mind. *At dawn the angels will sing and the doves will fly.* "What do you mean?" he asked the heavens. Arms stretched to the sky above. "What does that mean?"

He waited. This time he heard the beautiful sound of a harp. A harp. He'd heard a harp. He was sure he had to be hallucinating. It didn't surprise him after what he'd been through. He was hearing things. This was crazy. "At dawn the angels will sing and the doves will fly. It was ludicrous. Now harps were playing in the sky.

Nick decided he was having a nervous breakdown but would survive. Daylight would be here soon. He was going to be okay.

He ate another kaiser bun, curled into the fetal position and fantasized about being with Samantha. He could almost feel her straddle him, kissing him behind the ears and all over. He could feel her tongue run down the chest of his body. He could smell her body covered in oil. The scent of her perfume. He wondered why he'd left.

He thought about his brothers and wondered what they were doing. When he got out of this Hell he was going to have a big corn roast and invite everyone except Samantha so he could get really drunk. She hated it when he drank too much. She would be hurt and humiliated but he'd done it before.

The wind picked up and sent a chill through him. He curled up tighter and thought about a warm fire. He was sure the night was never going to end. He was probably going to freeze sitting in the cold, dark night, with the buzzards in the sky and the wind howling. He will surely die before dawn and the buzzards would eat him. His spirit would be stuck in this place forever. Even the military warned him it wasn't safe and to go home.

He lit his cigarette again, but it made him sick, queasy, and nauseated.

Again he heard planes in the distance.

He wanted to write a story above all stories that had ever been written. When his story hit the press and was read all over the world, he wanted it to solve world peace. That was his goal and ambition. It was big, and if he told anyone they would think he was nuts. He insisted he would persist until he succeeded. If it worked and he was successful then maybe Samantha would forgive him for being a jerk.

The night continued to drag. It was an endless, everlasting darkness. He checked his watch to find it was three a.m. He almost dreaded daylight because he would have to do something. Where was he going to go? What was he going to do? He didn't know.

A buzzard screeched.

Nick was sure he'd shoot the thing if he had a gun.

He started to think about the United Nations. They've been around since the Second World War when on January 1, 1943, then USA President Franklin Roosevelt used the term 'United Nations' to describe the 26 United Nations who joined together and pledged to fight against the Axis Powers. It was the declaration of the United Nations. The forerunner to the United Nations was the League of Nations, an organization conceived during the first World War for similar purposes. The United Nations needed to become more aggressive in the fight for human rights.

In 1995, 7,400 Muslim men and boys were massacred in the Bosnian town of Srebrenica, a supposedly UN safe area. The same thing happened in Rwanda in 1994 when 500,000 were left dead. "Thou shalt not kill," is one of the Ten Commandments.

He heard a rustling sound in the distant bush and his imagination went into overdrive. His heart began to pound hard and fast. It felt as though it would pop out of his chest. What was it? He curled up deeper into the rock beside him and hoped the noise wasn't something that was going to harm him. He visualized the maniacs with their swords and guns. He didn't want to end up like the ones in the hole.

He was freaking beyond comprehension. It was making him totally deranged. His life flashed before his eyes as the rustling sound came closer. He listened carefully, but it was dark. He didn't know if he was going to be able to fend for himself because he was weak. He didn't want to sacrifice himself to the holocaust of the mean-spirited-evil minds. Devil worshipers. Only people who work for the devil would do such things as he'd witnessed. His vulnerability toward it would last a lifetime. He would never forget. The crushing submersion of hate and hostility would end because he would see to it.

The sound was upon him, feet a way. Afraid to look, he cringed, opened his eyes, and looked up. His body dissolved in to a meltdown as he saw two beautiful baby foxes, happily playing together, running past.

He let out a sigh of relief and decided one day he would dedicate a story of recognition to the beautiful lowly fox.

He lay there shivering for the rest of the night, not sleeping a wink. The words going through his mind: *At dawn the angels will sing and the doves will fly.* And he'd heard a harp. No, he hadn't heard a harp. Impossible. It had to have been just another animal.

Everything was blurry and confusing. Thoughts were racing through his mind like the whirlwind of a hurricane. He was scared, lonely, and frightened. His body and soul ached in weariness beyond anything he'd ever experienced. He was disoriented and confused. The hawks were getting on his every nerve ending.

Thoughts of the politicians and the United Nations were rushing into his mind and his mood swung back and forth from a state of helplessness to a state of good fellowship.

This went on all night; over and over he bounced between these two moods. The hawks constantly screeching. An owl added to the chorus.

Finally he saw the first glimpse of twilight; a tiny speck of light coming up over the field. He stood to watch it. He waited. He wondered. It was dawn and he wasn't afraid any more because he was beyond intimidation. He felt a chilling sensation moving up and down the center of his spine. The horizon turned the most brilliant and unbelievable colors of pink, red, and yellow. There was a giant rainbow across the sky. It was like a fireball exploding in the morning mist. The beauty, sensationalism, and utter magnificence of the view stunned him. He'd never before witnessed such a spectacular array of color.

He heard it again. Harps. Faint at first, but they gradually become louder. He glanced around, jumped up, and spun in a circle.

He heard the voice again. "You can't see us, Nick."

He heard a choir. A sensation of melody. Suddenly birds were flying everywhere. Not birds. Doves. Beautiful white doves and hundred of them. White as white could be. It was surreal. He pinched himself because he was sure he was dreaming. He would wake up.

The sky radiated with sensation, the music was unbelievable, and doves were flying everywhere. It was a movie or something. Maybe he'd been abducted by aliens and taken somewhere because this was not earth. He must be hallucinating.

He closed his eyes for a second. When he opened them, the vision was still there. He pinched his leg. Yes, he *was* awake.

The emotion within him was unlike anything he'd ever experienced in this lifetime. He became perplexed and elated. A choir of angels was rejoicing in an exhilarating jubilation of joy and triumph.

Again, he heard a faint, quiet, little voice, "Nick."

He spun around. He could hear the music and voices, but couldn't see them. All that was visible was the incredible sky and doves flying everywhere.

"Nick, this is your sign. You asked God for a sign. It is the sign of peace. You must take this vision with you in your travels. Let this help you in your quest for peace, freedom and human rights."

Then the harp and the choir of angels played and sang the most inspirational sound he'd ever heard. There were no words, just voices harmonizing together in a victorious melody of tune and music.

It all just faded away.

He'd gone to Heaven and back.

Nick stood in a state of enthralled memoir to the dawn of the morning sun. It was just another day in Kosovo.

Chapter Two

Nick doesn't recall how long he stood there, but someone was shaking him.

"He's dazed and confused," one of the said.

"Looks like he's in some type of shock," the other one added.

He can hear them speaking, but couldn't respond. They were rummaging through his pack.

"Here's some I. D. He's a reporter for the *Weekly Tribute*."

Nick recognized the uniforms and the blue berets on their heads. The blue beret was the United Nation Peacekeepers. There were American flags on their shoulders. They were American Peacekeepers. What did they want with him? Why were they rummaging through his pack?

"Nick Sanders. Hey, Nick Sanders, what's going on with you? We're going to help you."

He couldn't respond. He was too dazed and baffled.

One of them grabbed his arm and started to tug. "Come with us, Nick, we're going to find you some help."

The peacekeepers looked at each other. "What do you think? Hospital?"

"Sure."

"Can you walk?"

Nick was staring off into nowhere land. He could still see the vision in the back of his mind. It wouldn't leave. What was it? What did it mean? What was he supposed to do with it? The words still echoing, "Take this vision with you in your quest for peace."

Oh no, he hadn't taken any pictures because he'd set his camera down. NO! He couldn't believe it. He'd missed getting it all on film. Even if he'd had his camera on, he probably wouldn't have taken any pictures anyway because he'd been too stunned. His brain had frozen. He probably wouldn't have been able to get that complex organ to function enough to have done it.

Wow, it had been beautiful. How he wished he'd gotten it on film. Oh well, no point in dwelling over the past. It sure had been an awesome sight. One that he'd never forget. What was he supposed to do with this beautiful and breathtaking vision? It had been an experience filled with peace, love, and happiness. He was a new man. He compared it to the vision that had almost driven him to insanity. The hole. The carcasses in the hole. Dead. The sight and the smell. He can't believe he'd taken a picture of horror, hate and violence of the most unthinkable kind, yet he'd missed a picture of the most beautiful vision on the face of the earth. God works in mysterious ways.

"What's wrong, Nick?" they were asking.

He couldn't respond.

Should he wait for another vision? He could just tell them to go away. If he did then he may never get out of here and the people who'd chased him may come back.

He could snap out of it. The peacekeepers were on the outside wall of his mind, the one that he knew he needed to escape.

"Come on, Nick, we're going to take you some place safe. Talk to us."

He wished they would leave him alone. Leave him at peace with his vision He needed to make a quick decision. One guy had his pack, the other was tugging on his arm. He could see their Jeep in the distance and vaguely made out someone smoking a cigarette. Cigarette. Yes, that is what he needed. "Smoke?" he asked.

They quit tugging at him, stared at each other, and grinned.

Nick reached into his shirt and pulled out a package. He decided to quit smoking forever. He still had four, so may as well finish them. He handed them to the army boys. "Cigarette?"

"Ah no, it's okay. You only have four."

"No, go ahead. I'm going to quit after this."

"Well, okay then."

"So what bring you to this neck of the woods?" Nick asked.

They laugh. "Making our rounds. We spotted your pack from the road. You looked baffled. You okay?"

"Fine." He took a drag on the smoke. "Did you see anything?"

"Like what? We see lots of stuff." They both laughed again. They were in pretty good humor for what was happening around them. "Did you like the sunrise this morning? Did you see the sunrise?"

"Oh sure, came up outside my window. It was pretty red this morning. You know what they say: red sky at night, sailor's delight. Red sky in the morn, sailors warn."

"Did you hear anything?"

"Just my roommate snoring."

"Hmmm," Nick mumbled. "So there was nothing unordinary about the sunrise this morning?

"Just bright. It was bright. Don't you think, Jeff?"

"Didn't see it. Was in the can around then. Why? What's the big deal?"

Nick thought about it and decided not to tell them. They would think he was crazy. "What are you guys doing today?"

Jeff and Rob looked at each other and laughed again. "Oh the usual. Making the rounds. Reporting any violence. You know, just the usual."

He looked at their guns slung across their shoulders.

"Do you want us to take you to the hospital or what?" Rob asked.

Nick thought for a minute. He might get a free bed and a hot meal, but he wasn't sure he wanted to go. He wanted to go, but was apprehensive about leaving his spot of weird spiritual encounter. "Have you been to that village over there?" He pointed into the direction from which he'd run.

"Not yet. It's on our rounds. There was some trouble over there yesterday. The British are there doing their thing."

Doing their thing. They made it sound like a trip to the outhouse.

"I was there," Nick said. "I saw it and photographed it. Some of them tried to kill me. They chased me for a while. I don't know how I ended up here, but it was a rough night."

"I'll bet. Did you say you have pictures?"

"Yes. I think so."

"That's good. Someone will want them."

"Have you ever wondered how someone could put a stop to it?"

"To what?"

"The killing. The hate."

"Oh, we wonder about that too. That's why we're here, to put a stop to it."

"They've successfully stopped the killing in Bosnia for the last couple of years using Micro UAV's," Jeff said. Have you heard of them?"

"Yes. They are micro miniature planes that the troops can launch and see what is going on. Little spy planes equipped with cameras and joysticks. Stuff like that. Now the Germans have developed a helicopter the size of a peanut."

"Why aren't they using them here?"

"Who knows?"

"They just curtail the killing. I'm talking about finding a way to stop it forever."

"Like a magic show, is that what you're talking about?"

The guy in the Jeep honked his horn. "You guys coming or what?" he yelled.

"You coming with us, Nick? It really isn't too safe out here. They're talking about another air strike."

"I'm thinking about it."

"Well, we're leaving and you're welcome to come. We'll drop you off at the hospital. First we have to stop at the village."

The village. The village. That is where it had happened. It was there at that place that the horror had gotten to him. If he stayed here, he'd probably die.

"Okay. Take me with you."

Rob picked up his pack and was startled by the weight. "What do you have in this thing?"

"The usual reporter stuff. Film, video camera, tape player, food, clothes. Heavy, aye?"

Rob nodded. After a few meters he handed it over to Jeff. "Lift this."

"Be careful with the thing," Nick begged.

They approached the Jeep.

The driver was sitting with his feet on the dashboard thinking about Vietnam and the time his two buddies were walking through a field like that and stepped on a land mine. He'd never forgotten the vision. It had been twenty years ago. Here he was, at it again. He loved the army, the travel, the adventure, but he hated the fighting. He was getting old.

Jeff carefully put Nick's pack in the back of the Jeep. "Okay, let's go."

They shared the usual chitchat when three beautiful white birds flew above the open Jeep.

Steven stopped suddenly in the middle of the road.

They sat in a state of shock.

Jeff finally said, "I've never seen pigeons that white before."

"Doves," Nick told them. "Doves. Member of the pigeon family."

They all watched in awe as they fluttered over head then flew away.

"Pretty," Jeff commented.

Nick wasn't surprised. "Are there many of them around here?" he asked, not mentioning his earlier encounter with them.

"Never seen ones like that," Steven said.

The other two shook their heads. "They are really beautiful birds."

Darn. He hadn't gotten a picture. "Wait a second. I want to get my camera." Nick requested. He jumped out of the Jeep, went to the back of the vehicle, grabbed his camera, an extra roll of film, and hot-rods. "Are you in a hurry?" he asked and looked through the lens.

He couldn't believe what he saw. Above the Jeep was an angel. It had wings and a white outfit. It was almost transparent and was fluttering above them. He clicked the shudder three times, seeing the angel in each frame.

"That should be good for the front cover."

The boys laughed as he climbed into the Jeep.

Nick didn't mention he'd seen angels.

They drove for what felt like an eternity until they arrived at the village. British troops were hauling bodies out of the hole.

Steven stopped the Jeep a few feet from the back of the British convoy.

Nick held tight to his camera, prepared for anything. After a few minutes an American solider came over to the side of the Jeep.

"Nice mess," Steve said.

"The boys are gagging big time."

He recognized the Captain stripes on his uniform. "I was here yesterday," Nick told him. "I saw it happen."

"You did. Good. I'll get a statement from you."

"I have pictures too. I can put people at the scene."

The soldier's eyes lit up. "Great. The United Nations is going to love you."

"Where were they yesterday when all this happened?"

"They can't be everywhere at once. Half the world is in a fight of some type. Forty people, including sixteen French peacekeepers were injured in Mitrovica yesterday."

"These people have been shot, stabbed and mutilated. Look in that pit," Nick yelled.

"Hey don't take your anger out on me. I didn't do it. We're just cleaning up the mess."

Nick paused. "Sorry, it baffles me as to why this is happening. What is wrong with these people?"

"Who knows? Let's talk about those pictures."

"They are still in the camera. I should finish the roll and then…" his voice trailed off as he saw the doves again. This time there were approximately a hundred of them headed in their direction. They simply appeared from nowhere.

Everyone paused and looked up.

Nick put his camera to his face; he wasn't going to miss them this time. Angels. He could see angels through it. He didn't believe it. He clicked the shudder button as fast as he could, taking five or six pictures. He pulled the camera away. No angels. He looked through the lens again. He saw angels and doves. He pulled the camera away and no angels. He took it from around his neck and handed it to Jeff who was sitting beside him.

"Look into this. Quick, look." He shoved the camera to his face.

Jeff gave the frantic Nick a puzzled look, grabbed the camera, put it to his eye, and looked at the birds.

"What do you see?

"Birds. Doves. Lots of them. Why?"

"You don't see anything really strange in that lens?"

"Besides birds, no."

Nick grabbed the camera and peered through the lens again. He saw angels and doves. "You only see birds and nothing else?"

"That's right."

Nick handed the camera over to the Captain. "You look."

The Captain tried. He gave Nick the same answer. "Doves. Wow, they are beautiful. I've never seen such beautiful birds before."

Everyone was bewildered at their sight. They were white as white could be.

"Give me that thing," Nick screamed. In a wild frenzy he photographed the birds. Once again he saw angels flying everywhere. He heard harps. He jumped out of the Jeep and moved to the open area. They were hovering above the hole with the bodies where the troops were working. They were hovering everywhere. They hovered above the workers wearing masks, outfits, tall boots, and gloves.

35

Nick photographed the people as they watched the birds. Again, through the camera, he saw angels. Then the harps strummed. The angels sang.

"Hear that?" Nick asked.

"The fluttering?" Yes, they sure do flutter a lot."

"No. The music and the singing."

"Right," Jeff said.

They seriously examined him.

"You don't hear it?"

Everyone was stunned and confused.

"The singing. The harp and the angels singing."

"No, Nick, we don't hear anything. Why? Do you?" Steve asked.

Nick's shoulders slumped. He was crazy. Either he was crazy or something strange was happening. Why would God send angels and harps for only him?

He heard a little voice, "They are non-believers. Only you believe. Only you can do this."

"Do what?" Nick turned toward the voice, but no one was there.

"Take these visions with you in your journey for human rights."

"What journey?" he yelled.

Everyone looked at Nick who had just shouted at no one.

There was no answer. The music and singing stopped. The doves flew away. There were a few moments of silence, then everyone began to talk about what they'd just seen.

Nick figured he was going crazy. Was he or wasn't he? What the heck was going on with his mind? He was losing it. He had to get the film developed and now.

"You want those pictures? Find me a lab."

"Just give me the film," the Captain said.

"No way. I go where it goes. Let me finish this roll."

As he was walking away, a solider came over to the captain. "We've collected everything that resembles a corpse. The rest are limbs. Okay for a mass grave?"

"Be sure to keep all heads."

The solider glanced back at him, probably hoping it was the end of digging through the stench and horror. "Certainly, sir." He walked away.

Nick sauntered over to the grave and gagged. The infamous blackbirds and wild dogs were everywhere, circling the site, acting like vultures, waiting to move in on the prey.

As best as he could, and choking back his gag, he began to take pictures. Again, each time he saw angels in the camera.

This was definitely the most hated moment of his life. He hoped he never had to do anything like this ever again.

He took several shot of the bodies that they hauled out of the hole. Again, angels were fluttering above them.

The blood, stench, and horror on the corpse's faces were awful. Children, women, and men; an entire village wiped out.

Slowly and methodically he turned and walked away.

He popped his head in the door at the Red Cross bus where a nurse was treating a gouge in a woman's arm.

"Can I ask you something?"

The nurse looked at him briefly. "Sure."

"Did you see angels and hear harps when those doves flew through?"

The nurse laughed. "Oh sure. I saw Santa Claus too."

"Never mind."

He could sense the boys talking about him when he returned to the Jeep.

"So you saw the entire thing?" the Captain quizzed him again. "Tell me about it."

Nick looked at him. He really didn't want to do this. "Can't you just read about it when I'm finished?"

"*NO. NOW!*" he shouted.

Nick was afraid he would haul him in. "Okay, okay."

"Sorry, but I have a report to file and so far you're the only eyewitness."

"Okay. So, I was over there." With trembling hands he pointed to a little store. "I had just come out of that store when I saw the rebels marching down that road." He pointed in the opposite direction. "So I went back into the store and took a few pictures from that window, then took off out back and hid in that cluster of bush, taking more pictures." He gasped for breath. "They were going into homes and businesses, grabbing people, and leading them over to that ravine. That's where it all happened." He was pointing at the site.

The captain nodded.

"A couple of them started coming this way so I took off." The grizzly words bit into him as he spoke.

"They chased me for a while, but I was really booting it. I kept running and running until I landed at some rock. That's when these guys found me the next morning."

"You outran them with that pack?"

"Yup. I used to play football in high school." Nick grinned.

"You're lucky you didn't trip on a landmine, they're all over the place."

"I know. I was afraid of that."

The captain was taking notes. "That's it?"

That's it. What more did he want? Nick nodded his head. He hoped that *really* was it.

"Let's get to a lab. Where are you guys going?" he asked the driver.

Steve gave him their detail. "Making rounds. We make rounds every day and report back to the Sarge."

"Well, we're going to a lab. I don't want to lose this guy."

"Sure. We can do that. You let our sergeant know what we're up to."

"Hold on a second. I need to deal with a few things first. I'll be back."

"Sure, take all the time you need," Steve told him as he walked away.

They silently sat in the Jeep, waiting.

Nick's stomach growled. "I need a good chow down."

"I'll get you something," Rob said, hopped out of the Jeep, and headed for the food bus.

"I'll go with you." Jeff jumped up and followed him.

Nick sat silently in the back of the Jeep. Steve turned and looked at him. "Are you okay?"

"Somewhat. As best as can be expected, considering everything. I'll be better when I get something to eat." He was stunned and perplexed by the spiritual encounter. He really did think he might be losing his mind. "Have you ever had a nervous breakdown?"

"Oh, a few. Isn't hard in this field."

"What happens to you?"

"To me?"

"To anyone."

"Everyone is different. No two nervous breakdowns are ever the same. The same person never has the same breakdown twice. Everyone is different. Different degrees. Why?"

"Oh, Ah, Just. Ah, last night something happened to me."

"What?"

"I'm not sure. Let's just say it was an interesting night. So…what happens to you when you break down?"

"Well, I've never really had it get to me so bad that a few stiff drinks wouldn't cure it, but one night in Vietnam I was sure I was going to lose it. They had us pinned behind a wall for days. We nearly died, in fact a few did die and, well, my nerves were so fried you could hear them sizzling. It was a long couple of days. We've had people lose their minds so bad they need hospitals and drugs. Some people never recover, but that's in extreme cases. They range from mild to severe. Basically, it's just stress overload. People really need a lot of positive, emotional support at that time. Exercise sometimes can fix it, providing the person isn't physically exhausted. If they're exhausted, then they need rest and lots of it."

Rob and Jeff came back with a mountain of food.

"Wow," Nick said as Rob threw him a sub sandwich.

"That girl was real nice to us when I told her we had a hungry witness."

"Yeah, she didn't even ask to see our ration cards."

They handed Steve a cup of coffee. He took a sip and spit it out. "You did it again. I can't drink this shit." He handed it back. "That'll make me puke, all that sugar."

Rob and Jeff laughed. "Oops, wrong one." He handed him the unsweetened one.

Steve flashed an ear to ear smile. "Thanks." He happily tore off the lid.

A group of French peacekeepers came toward the Jeep.

Nick grabbed his camera and took a few shots of them. His eye caught a cute female. "Hey," he shouted. "One minute for some pictures."

The gang turned to look.

The girl had the most fantastic photogenic face. Her hair neatly tied in a bun. He had to catch it on film. She smiled at him as he clicked away. She was a beautiful vision in a troubled day.

"You. Please, go stand beside that tree there," he politely asked her.

"Who me?" She turned. Her bright, sparkly, eyes warmed him.

"Yes. Yes. You. Please let me take your picture."

The girl smiled. Several males yelled something to her in French. They whistled. They worked for the family identification program. It was their job to name the corpses and notify the families. Not a fun job but they were trained to deal with it. It was better than digging holes.

Everyone had a chuckle. The little release of laughter felt good.

The girl walked over to the tree. "Why me?"

"Because you have the face of an angel. Just look natural."

She stood beside the tree. Nick looked into his camera and there she was again, hovering over the girl, fluttering above her, that angel. He snapped a couple shots and turned toward the boys in the Jeep. "Come look into this and tell me what you see."

Steve carefully took the camera and held it up to his face. "She's a beauty, no doubt about it."

"But do you see anything strange?"

Steve looked again. "Just a gorgeous woman. What's so strange about that?"

"You don't see anything unusual?"

"Well, I'm not very good with the camera. The light is good."

Nick took the camera from him and peered through the lens. The angel was still there.

He took five or six more shots, let the camera fall around his neck, took out his notebook, and got her name, rank, and platoon. "Merci," he told her.

She said something in French that he didn't understand, gave him a warm gentle smile and walked to join her friends. He watched her sexy butt for a minute, mesmerized by her.

Simple beauty and radiance. It would be a good picture for sure. No one was going to believe his pictures when he got them developed.

Finally they saw the captain heading their way.

Steve started the Jeep and drove the ten feet to pick him up. "Everything okay?"

"Fine. The identification process is hard. Dealing with the families is even harder. The French are looking after that, they have a well-trained gang to deal with it."

"We just met them. I'll just radio my sergeant," Steve said, and picked up the hand-piece.

"We're going to Pristina," he told him, speaking into the crackly device.

"The fuck you are," he bellowed. "Get back to work."

Steve knew there was no sense trying to talk to him because he had his nose so far up his ass that he rarely listened to his subordinates. He was the type of sergeant who should be shoveling paper, not giving commands. Steve handed the hand set over to the captain. "You talk to him."

The captain took it. "This is Captain Smith from the 23rd U.S. Battalion. Michigan. I have solicited the assistance of your driver and patrol Jeep to take me to Pristina. I have a valuable witness with a roll of film and we're in a big hurry."

"And where is your own driver? I need those guys to be making rounds. They're not chauffeurs, they're on patrol. Now I'm telling you to find your own ride."

Everyone rolled their eyes.

Jeff let out a smirk.

"Not possible. There was another slaughter in Devin last night and they're dealing with it. There is no one available right now."

"You can't drive yourself?"

"No vehicle, thank you."

"You'll be on report to the general for this," the sergeant bellowed.

"Fine," Captain Smith said. He turned the radio off.

Rob and Jeff chuckled. The sergeant was a jerk. They really didn't like him too much.

Nick pulled out his cigarette package and peered inside. He had exactly two. He lit one. "This is going to be the second last cigarette I will ever smoke in my life. I have one left and after this, that's it."

"Oh sure," Jeff said. "The last time I quit smoking was ten minutes ago."

The road was bumpy and poorly maintained, but it was beautiful mountainous countryside.

Nick enjoyed the scenery, snapping pictures. A couple ferrets ran across the road. "Stop," Nick said. "Let me take their picture."

Steve glanced back quickly. "Nick, this isn't CBC news mobile you know. I don't mind stopping for something really amazing, but come on, ferrets?"

"They don't run wild where I come from. People keep them in cages and raise them for the fur. I just thought it could be an interesting side bar, Ferrets in Kosovo."

"Ferrets in Kosovo! Don't you work for the *Tribute*?" Rob asked.

"Yeah, why?"

"I didn't know they printed unimportant stuff like that. I thought it was just a news magazine."

"When I become editor-in-chief, it's going to expand to include a light reading section. Helps people take their mind off all the awful crap that's going on everywhere."

Everyone was silent. No one liked what they were doing, but it was a paycheck. They did their jobs, enjoyed whatever adventures they could from the travel, and hoped they didn't get poisoned by some chemical, step on a land mine, or get hit with a bullet or missile. When it was over, they would go home a different person—colder and harder. Only the really tough survive. If you were lucky enough to survive it physically and emotionally, you could continue on with your life. Then do it all again. As far as Nick was concerned, once a military person signs on the dotted line they become a hero, each and everyone.

"Have you heard anything about that uranium report the UN was working on?" Steve asked the captain.

"Well NATO has admitted to using depleted uranium weapons here back in March which exposed civilians, troops and aid workers to health hazards. But the head of the UN Balkan Environmental task force investigating their use during that seventy-day war claims NATO is holding back data on where and how it used the weapons."

"That stuff will contaminate land and water with radioactive and toxic particles," Steve said.

"Oh sure, and the big question now is if it was also used in Siberia, Montenegro and other areas."

"How do they use uranium?" Nick wondered.

"The shells are tipped with depleted uranium to help them penetrate the thick armor of military vehicles or underground bunkers," the Captain told them. "In the 1991 Gulf War in Iraq there was a high epidemic of cancer among Iraqis living near battlefields where they used the stuff. Here in Kosovo they only used about one tenth of the amount they used over there. U.S. and British veterans of the Gulf War with Iraq have also blamed serious health problems on the use of them."

Nick gagged. "And…"

"The link is denied by U.S. and British military authorities."

"Of course," Nick commented. He sank into his seat, wishing he'd recorded the conversation. He made some notes, scribbling down 'health problems linked to uranium.'

He thought about Samantha just to get his mind off everything. He missed the way she excited him. The massages in the hot tub, the candlelight dinners, romance by the fire, dancing in the moonlight and the sex. Oh, the thought of sweet sex. They had the greatest sex life. He wondered how long she would mope over him before she realized he was not what she needed. She needed a man who could give her stability and security. He needed his financial and emotional freedom. He knew she really loved him, but he couldn't give her what she needed. Besides, she hated *The Simpsons* on TV. How could he date someone who hated *The Simpsons*?

They rode in silence for a while. It was almost as if everyone wanted to savor the momentary tranquility. So many thoughts were going through Nick's mind.

"Where are you from Nick?" Rob asked, breaking the utter stillness.

"Ontario, Canada. Small town. Very small.

"Sounds neat."

"It's a neat place if you like rocks and trees. It's really quiet and is host to one of the most toxic waste sites in North America. But that's okay because it's downstream from us. It flows through a creek that eventually feeds into Lake Ontario."

"Oh, and what is buried there?"

"All kinds of crap, including the residue from the bomb that bombed Hiroshima."

Everyone cringed.

They passed a pregnant woman pushing a stroller with a small baby.

"Wow. Look at the knockers on her. I'd love to suck one of them," Jeff said and turned around slurping.

"Hey," the captain yelled at him. "One more comment like that and you'll be on report."

"Sorry. Got carried away."

Everyone was taken back by the whole scenario.

Nick chuckled quietly to himself. He would like to suck titty right now, but there were too many important things to do. Samantha would let him suck her tits any time she wanted. She loved it when he did it and often she'd shove her knockers in his face. She was a horny thing and could probably put him in the cardiac wing if he wasn't careful.

"Why do you have the Canadian Flag on your knapsack?" the very tall Jeff asked.

Nick laughed. Stupid question. "I'm proud of my heritage. What condition is Pristina in?"

"It's a mess. A big mess. It's going to take a while to rebuild their infrastructure."

"Are the air strikes over yet?"

"Who knows? We hear something different every day. After what happened here in Devin yesterday, they'll probably continue."

"Are we going to be safe in Pristina?"

"I think so. Last thing I heard was to stay clear of Belgrade."

"That makes sense. They've been hitting the same targets over and over all over Kosovo. Tanks, buildings, stuff like that. They should have gone after Milosevic in Belgrade in the first place."

"This has been going on for two months now. Is it ever going to end?"

"We're not sure. There were close to one-million refugees in Macedonia and Albania. So far about seven-thousand have gone to Canada."

The scenery was nice. The mountains provided them with a picturesque backdrop.

Nick tried to enjoy the ride.

He wondered where he'd found the nerve to be doing what he was doing. He could die any minute. He thought about the young family he'd interviewed: the mother, father, and a small baby, who'd been ordered out of the house in five minutes by Servian militiamen or be shot. They'd spent the night and next day outside in the rain until they were ordered at gunpoint onto a train to be shipped to a refugee camp. Hitler rides again. They ordered Nick to leave the country as well. He told them he was on his way, thinking they were going to shoot him. He was surprised they'd let him go. It had been another terrifying moment in his visit to this ravished country. Ravished by war. It was sad, really sad.

Jeff handed everyone a mangled, squished brownie that he pulled out of the side pocket of his trousers. The chocolate almost gave Nick an oral orgasm.

He couldn't wait to see his pictures, to feel them, hold them, and show them to Jack who was going to love him. Maybe he'd give him a bonus. He decided to prepare the boys for the truth. "There are angels on this roll of film."

There was silence. Little grins spread on everyone's face.

"And what pictures would you be referring to?" Rob asked.

"The roll in the camera. Almost every picture I took since I left the rock this morning has an angel in it.

"Oh, they do. That's nice."

"Seriously. You didn't see them? No one saw angels? Come on guys, tell me the truth, you did see angels, right?"

The boys had difficulty finding the words. In situations like this, some theories say to play along with the dementia. Others say to tell them the truth. The problem was that what worked for one person didn't always work for the other.

"Did you see angels Steve?" the Captain asked the driver.

"No, I didn't see angels. Did you?"

"Well, there are angels on this roll of film. I saw them and I took pictures of them."

"Good. We need angels." Jeff added.

"You'll see."

"Do you still want to go to the hospital, Nick?" Rob asked. "To get checked out or something?"

Nick thought for a minute. He didn't need the hospital, but he was sure he could use the rest. "Maybe. Let's get the film developed."

"Did you hear what happened the other day with the tractor?" Steve asked.

"Tractor, no what tractor?"

"NATO mistook a tractor full of refugees for a tank and killed seventy-five refuges."

"Crap. That's not good."

"I heard they took out the Sevian Police headquarters the other day."

"What are the Canadians flying?" An angel flew by as he asked. Nick took out his notebook.

"CF 18 jet fighters."

"How many?"

"Right now, twelve. But we heard your Prime Minister is sending six more."

"So, how many altogether?"

"They have a strike force of up to fifty planes between the Dutch, the Americans and the British."

"What are they dropping?"

"They were using five-hundred pound bombs, but now they're dropping two-thousand pounds."

"How are they directed?"

"Laser."

"Where are they stationed?"

"Italy."

"That's a long way."

"Two hour flight down the Adriatic Sea. They refuel midair over the water. It's the SAM's they're worried about."

"SAM's? What are SAM's?"

"Surface to air missiles. But apparently they aren't having any trouble seeing them."

"I was talking to a Canadian pilot who told me they had two Yugoslav jet fighters come at them and two Dutch f-16s intercepted them. They hit one and the other flew away. The pilot was stunned, said it happened so fast. Meanwhile his wife watched the horrific event on TV back home."

"It must be hard for them, dropping those things."

"Not really. They don't see eyes like the army guy does. They just see things: buildings, tanks, bridges, dams. It's all very technological."

Technological. What was life coming to? We blow each other up and call it technological. It was too much. "How much further?"

"We just passed a sign. Forty-five kilometers."

"Good."

Chapter Three

They drove the remaining distance in silence. Finally Pristina was in sight, a city with a population of one-hundred and eight-thousand. The commercial and transportation center for the surrounding mining region. There were numerous manufacturing firms, which included processed foods, jewelry, textiles, metals, wooden goods, and pharmaceuticals.

As they drove on the overpass, they found a city in rubble.

Steve pulled into a gas station to fill up.

Rob and Jeff went into the store and retrieved directions to a lab. There was a camera store a few blocks away.

Nick was excited.

The destruction was everywhere. The entire country had pretty much been decimated. All major buildings had been leveled or destroyed, bringing the city to third world standards.

Nick spied a coffee shop. "I'll be right back. I need a strong brew." He jumped out of the Jeep. "Keep an eye on my pack."

Once outside, he pulled the lid off the cup and sipped the steamy hot coffee. He pulled out his cigarettes, took a long look at his last, and lit it. He swore to himself that this was going to be his very last smoke.

"Nick, come on, what are you doing?" the captain yelled.

Nick held his camera close to his body, protecting it from nothing. "This is the very last cigarette that I'm ever going to smoke in my life. I want to savor it."

"Oh, for crying out loud, Nick, get your butt over here, we don't have all day."

"My life might change after I get that film developed, so I'm just saying goodbye to my old life."

"Whatever. You have one minute to get in the Jeep, then I'm hauling you in at gunpoint."

Jeff and Rob snickered. "Angels. He's going to show us angels." They both laughed.

"Keep your voices down," Steve said. "The guy is obviously sick. He probably just isn't used to this type of thing."

"So who is? I don't see angels and hear harps. Do you?"

"No, but just humor him. Once we get the film developed we can drop him off at the hospital."

Rob and Jeff were laughing.

Nick knew it was about him. He didn't care. He savored his last puff as he made one of the strongest convictions in his life; giving up his smokes. He threw the butt on the ground, stomped on it, grinding it to a pulp. He stared at it.

"What's he doing? Okay, time's up, Nick. Let's go. Let's do this. What is he staring at?"

"His cigarette butt."

"What's wrong with him?"

"At least he's talking and coherent. This morning when we found him, he was in shock."

"He did witness something awful, so it's to be expected I guess."

Nick looked up at the boys. "Okay, I'm ready."

The directions were correct. The shop was closed but in great shape as it was far from any destruction. They found the owner upstairs waiting for the war to end. He was happy to be of assistance in this important military matter.

Nick carefully unwound his film, hoping it wasn't a bad roll. That'd been known to happen. He handed it over to the shopkeeper.

"Give me an hour."

"Nothing doing. I'm coming with you," he demanded. "Someone else come with us." Nick wanted a witness. "Don't screw it up," he told the excited shopkeeper.

He watched him pulled the film into a long stretch and hooked it onto a machine that would feed it through another machine.

"You can watch them come out at the other end."

Nick was sure the clock had stopped. Finally the tip of the first picture appeared. It slid into the slot. Nick picked it up. It was a ruined building. He watched as a few more of the same building came out. There were crying children with torn clothing who he'd assisted. They'd been looking for their parents, so he'd found a sweet lady who was willing to help. Then the ones from the slaughter. They were clear enough. There were several. Hopefully enough for a conviction.

"These will work," Rob commented as he looked over his shoulder. "The captain is going to like them."

"Just wait." Nick held his breath because he knew what should be next and yes there they were. *Yes! Yes!* His camera had caught them on film. Nick was ecstatic. First there were the four pictures he'd taken of Rob, Jeff and Steve in the Jeep when they'd first picked him up and the angel was hovering above them. "Check these out."

Rob reached out his hand to grab them.

Nick pulled them back. "Don't touch anything."

Rob looked at the pictures as Nick held them. "Some kind of trick photography, right? Double lens or something?"

"No. These are for real. Go get the rest of the gang."

Rob yelled to the boys who were flipping through fashion magazines in a small sitting area. "Come and check out these pictures. You won't believe your eyes."

They followed him to the back room.

Nick continued to watch them fall from the machine. There were six shots of the grave site that he'd taken from the Jeep when they first returned to Devin. Among the doves were dozens of angels flying everywhere. The pictures were absolutely beautiful.

By now everyone was lingering over the machine, including the storekeeper, watching as the pictures dropped one by one into the slot.

"Don't touch them," Nick yelled again as the captain reached his hand in. "Leave them alone."

No one said anything as the rest of the pictures fell in to place. There were five shots of the grave site. In each one angels were hovering above them. Then out came the shots of the bodies on the ground. Angels were hovering over the bodies. Finally, the shots of the French Peacekeeper, an angel was hovering over her head.

Nick was incredibly happy. This was the proof he needed, if not for anyone but for himself. He wasn't insane.

"How did you do it, Nick?" the captain asked.

"Do what? I didn't do anything, these are for real." He looked at the clerk. "Make me triple prints please and another set of negatives."

"Sure thing."

"No one touches those pictures until copies are made."

After the third set was completed, Nick grabbed them and went over to the empty table where he sorted them out. He gave the Captain the ones from the slaughter. "The rest are mine."

The clerk wanted copies.

"Sorry, but these are exclusively for the magazine I work for."

Steve flipped through them as everyone huddled around. Slowly, carefully and unbelievably they were examined by all. "Okay, so tell us already. How did you do it? Special camera?"

"I'm telling you these are for real. Hey, this is nothing, you should've been with me at sunrise this morning."

"Sunrise? What happened at sunrise?"

"Forget it, you wouldn't believe me anyway."

"These are sensational. Do you still want a ride to the hospital?" Steve asked.

"Might just as well, I guess."

They arrived at the dilapidated hospital and stopped at the door.

Nick thanked everyone for their hospitality. They agreed to stay in touch. "I'll send you complimentary copies of the story," Nick promised.

"Do you want some help checking in?" Rob asked. "We can get you admitted pretty quick."

Nick thought for a minute. It had been a long couple of weeks. He was really exhausted. "Sure, that would be great."

Rob took him into the lobby. "Just make out like you're in major shock."

To their surprise the admission nurse spoke English.

Rob told her an over-exaggerated story about his condition.

The nurse did the necessary paperwork and admitted him right away.

Outside, Rob found the boys questioning the authenticity of the pictures.

"Maybe they are real, who knows? He did look really messed up this morning when we found him. Maybe he's on some type of mission."

"Mission. Right. You can get trick camera lenses. He rigged those pictures and you know it," the captain replied.

"I don't know," Rob added.

"Yeah. I've never seen anything like it," Jeff responded.

Chapter Four

"Let me take your pack," the cute nurse offered.

"No. It's okay. I'll carry it. I've a lot of valuable equipment."

"So you've been through quite an ordeal from the sound of things. We're used to dealing with that. I'll show you to your room. The doctor is making rounds. He'll be by soon to see you."

"Where did you learn to speak such great English?"

"My mother is from England. I was born here. She always insisted I speak English to her."

The nurse led him down a long hall.

He almost felt guilty when he saw the severity of people needing care. Men with legs and faces that had been blown off, arms gone.

Nick held up his camera. "May I?"

Julie asked her patients.

Everyone agreed to be photographed.

Nick cautiously clicked a few shots. He felt honored when the nurse led him to a private room.

"You probably need a good night's sleep, so I'll give you this room for now. I can't promise you how long you can have it, but for tonight it'll be okay."

"Thank you."

"Just put your pack here." She pointed to a chair.

"No, I want to keep it close by. I'll put it under the bed."

"Sure, whatever. Is there anyone you would like me to phone for you?"

Nick thought about Samantha and Jack, but decided they were on a need to know basis. They didn't need to know. For now anyway.

"I'll be okay. Thanks."

"Well, if you change your mind, let me know. Sometimes it can really help, reaching out to someone close." She checked his blood pressure.

"What I really need is rest. I was up all night alone in the bush, it was a bit scary."

Julie raised her eyebrows. "If you need someone, ring that bell. We're really busy, so please ring only if it's really necessary." She had a cute little smile.

Nick watched her lips move. She was young, beautiful, and petite. Her long, thick, dark hair was braided down her back

"Just doing my job. Do you want a pain killer?"

A painkiller. That was the last thing on his mind. Maybe a cigarette and a bottle of Jack Daniels. "What kind of painkiller?"

"Tylenol or something stronger. I can give you Tylenol, but the doctor has to order anything stronger."

Nick decided he didn't need to get all drugged up; he wanted to keep a clear mind. "Not right now, but I'll let you know if I change my mind." Something moved inside him as she gazed into his eyes. "What's your name?"

"Julie. Well, get in that bed," she ordered then left the room.

Nick climbed onto the bed, and as anticipated, it felt great. He hadn't had a good night's sleep since he'd left Vancouver. He'd been sleeping everywhere and anywhere. One night he slept in the back seat of a car and was worried all night that the owners would show up and shoot him.

Slowly he felt the aches and pains exit his body.

He needed a plan for the pictures. He wasn't sure what he needed to do with them. Obviously he was in touch with the spiritual world or something. He simply didn't know where to go or what to do next. The longer he lay, the more he realized the weariness that was upon him. This was neither the time nor place to be timid and weak.

He looked at the pictures again and again, studying each one. It was the same angel in all of them. She was hovering over the Jeep, amongst the angels at the grave site, and was with the French Peacekeeper. The angels were translucent. You could almost see right through them.

Drowsiness overcame him. He slipped into a deep slumber. The pictures fell from his hands.

Julie returned a few hours later with a dinner tray. She looked at her patient, who was peacefully sleeping and decided not to disturb him. She put his tray on the side table, turned to leave, and noticed pictures in his lap.

Carefully she picked them up and glanced at them casually. Then, with disbelief, she analyzed them. They were amazing and beautiful. She wondered if they were authentic. They weren't clouds. What were they? One was nothing but doves and angels. It was of most incredible beauty. She was baffled. A sensation ran down her spine. Authentic or not, these were the most bewildering photographs she'd ever see. They were magnificent. What did they stand for? What was it all about? They were a contrast of circumstance; beauty amongst the horror. How had he done it? Why had he done it? Why had he created such sensational work? What was going on in this guy's brain? He was a photojournalist; she knew that, but why create such images?

She flipped through them one last time then carefully placed them on the table beside his dinner tray.

She watched him sleep. He was an attractive man with a sincere smile. His graying, black, curly hair gave him a distinguished air. She wondered about him. Where had he grown up? What had his childhood been like? He had a beautiful body, tad overweight, but solid. Well built and beautifully shaped. She was attracted to this foreigner.

She crept out of the room, stopping for one more glance at the sexy body in the bed.

Nick jumped up and for a minute he was confused as to where he was. Surveying his surroundings he remembers he's in the hospital. Glancing at his watch, he's surprised to find it's five in the morning.

He'd slept for almost twelve hours. He remembered the pictures.
Where were the pictures?

In a panic, he rummages through his bed. He takes a deep sigh of
relief when he spied the pile on the table. He fell back on the bed,
totally exhausted. He was glad he was in the hospital because he
didn't want to be alone. Vision of the horror began to sink in. His
nerves were feeling red raw.

He glanced under the bed to check that his pack is still there and
took another sigh of relief when he found it.

Getting up to urinate, he stumbles out of bed and realizes he's
exhausted. He can barely walk. Mentally and physically he's spun
out. He sits down on the toilet so not to lose his balance, pees for an
eternity then shakes off the drops. While washing his hands, he
glanced in the mirror. His bloodshot eyes revealed most of the story.
The bags tell the rest. He needed more sleep. Back in his room, he
glanced at the food on his tray. It was stew. Not knowing how long
it'd been there, he picked out the vegetables and left the meat. It
tasted really good, so he ate the stale roll and drank the sour juice.
Even the lousy water tasted okay.

Glancing through his pictures, he felt as though he was seeing
them for the first time.

He climbed back in bed, fell asleep and dreamt about Samantha.
In his dreams she always wore a long flowing gown, her long hair
flying everywhere.

A heavyset, short, older nurse was standing over the bed. "Mr.
Saunders. The doctor is here to see you."

Nick opened his eyes to find the doctor looking down at him. A
kind, elderly face. The blood on his shirt made him cringe, reminding
him of the bodies in the ditch.

"How are you today, Mr. Saunders?"

"You can call me Nick."

"How are you today, Nick?"

Nick looked at him, carefully choosing his words. He needed
more rest, therefore he wanted to ensure he wasn't discharged today.
"Awful. And I have a really bad hemorrhoid."

"Hemorrhoid. Well, roll over and let me look."

Nick removed his pants and turned over.

"Ouch, I guess you do. How did you get that?"

"Sitting on a rock for about twelve hours."

"That would do it. I'll order you some cream. I hear you've been through a traumatic experience. Can I get you something to relax?"

Nick was thinking about a big bottle of whisky. Anyway, the pictures proved he wasn't crazy, so he wasn't overly worried about that any more. Before seeing the pictures, he thought maybe, just maybe, he was a bit touched in the head. Now he knew he wasn't.

"I'm not exactly sure exactly what it is I need, doctor."

"Well, try to rest. I'll return later to check on you." He turned to leave and saw the pictures on the table. "May I?"

"Sure. Go ahead."

Nick watched the expression on his face. He was obviously intrigued.

"These are very interesting. How'd you do it?"

"Do what? They're real. I didn't do anything. They *are* the real thing."

The doctor looked at him.

Nick could see the wheels churning in his brain.

"Well, they're beautiful." He put them down. "I'll be back later. Get some more rest." He left the room.

Nick was certain the doctor didn't believe him. He wondered if anyone was going to believe him.

The overweight nurse came back with the breakfast tray and placed in on the table. She too asked to look at the pictures.

"Sure. Why not?" He devoured his bacon and eggs. Breakfast never tasted so good.

"These are really good. Double negatives right? I know how you do that. You place two negatives on the same picture. Neat."

"No, they *are* real. I didn't do anything with the negatives. In fact, the guy in the photo shop printed them up. Ask him. Actually, I have the negatives right here." He reached down and pulled out his pack, unzipped the front pouch and pulled out an envelope. He held them up to the light. "Look." He handed one to the nurse.

She looked at it in the light. "Amazing."

"Where's Julie?"

"She'll be here at three."

"Is she attached?"

"Her boyfriend was killed last year in a clash. She really hasn't gotten over it. Her parents have fled to Europe for safety. She's basically alone right now. I don't know why she stays."

Nick knew why, she was a humanitarian. Most nurses are.

"Is there a phone I can use? I need to call my boss."

"There's a payphone in the lobby. Sometimes it works."

The lobby seemed a hundred miles away. "Thanks."

"There's a shower down the hall if you want. I'll get you a towel."

Nick smiled. The thought of a shower made him happy, but he didn't think he had the energy for it right now. He was really tired. "Thanks."

"Is there anything else you need?"

"Just rest." He watched her leave the room. He wondered what he was going to do with the pictures.

"The Canadian wants to know if you're single," Nurse Andrea asked Julie at shift change.

"He does!" Her eyes lit up.

"What did you tell him?"

"The truth."

Thinking about the truth was painful.

"Did you see his pictures?"

"The ones with weird doves and angels in them?"

"Yes, those ones. Beautiful."

"He claims they're real. He showed me the negatives. I still think he rigged them."

Julie didn't answer. She'd worked with the mentally disturbed before and had learnt to keep an open mind about everything. If they tell you a story that is unbelievable, it just could be true. "How's he doing?"

"I'm not sure. One of the soldiers that brought him in called and told us he was really out of it yesterday morning when they found him."

"Doesn't surprise me. He witnessed something really awful."

Julie knocked quietly on Nick's door and peered inside. Her handsome patient appeared to be sleeping. She approached his bed.

"Nick. Can I take your blood pressure?"

Nick smiled up at her and held out his arm. "I need artificial respiration too."

"Funny." She wrapped the apparatus around his muscular arm and pushed the little bulb.

"So?"

"Little bit high, but nothing to worry about."

Nick smiled.

"I hear you were asking about me?"

"Uh huh."

"And how about you, Mr. Saunders? Someone as good looking as you must have a woman somewhere."

Nick remembered the long line of women he'd had in his forty-six years. There'd been a few, but no one had loved him like Samantha.

"Well?"

"Well there's a girl back home who's in love with me. But it'll never work."

Julie studied him carefully. She didn't need a broken heart. "How long are you staying in the country?"

"Not sure exactly. I was supposed to be home yesterday, but that's not possible. I need to call my boss because I want to stay longer."

"Oh."

"Do you know anything about Slobodan Milosevic?"

"He's a monster. He's the Serbian President, the one responsible for all the horror. Why?"

"Just wondering."

"NATO dropped a bunch of bombs in Belgrade last night." she told him.

"They did? Do you know anything about the United Nations?" Nick wanted people's opinions on everything.

"What about them?"

"What do you know about them?"

"Not much, only that they've let us down before. But they're not always safe themselves. Serb forces overran the town of Srebrenica in August 1995, despite being declared a UN safe area. They killed two-thousand people there. Putting on a peacekeeping uniform doesn't always protect you."

Nick thought about it. She was right, the United Nations weren't magicians. He looked into her eyes and visualized her naked body. He felt his penis grow. He shifted his body, hoping she wouldn't notice his boner. He wanted her. He wanted to throw her down on the bed and make out with her. He didn't have the energy to do it, but it would be nice.

"I have to get back to work. If you need anything, just ring."

"Can you help me have a shower?"

Julie smiled. "It's just down the hall. You don't really need help, *do you?*"

"I'm not sure if my balance is okay. I was a bit dizzy earlier."

"I have wounds to dress. I'll come back later."

Her words excited him. He watched her exit the room. She was graceful, elegant, petite, and strong. She was a beauty in a world of hate.

He craved a cigarette, but was determined those days were over for good. His throat began to hurt. He felt he might be on the verge of losing his voice.

He racked his brain trying to decide what to do next. The words he'd heard in the bush echoed in his memory. The vision was causing the electrical circuits in his brain to fire. He could almost feel it happening. "Take this vision with you in your travels and let it help you in your quest for peace, freedom and human rights." What did it mean? He decided to ask God once again for help.

"Dear God, please help me. I do not know what to do with the vision you sent. I do not know what to do with the pictures. I do not know what to do with the politicians and the United Nations. Please, dear God, I need more help. What am I suppose to do?"

He waited, got out of bed, and looked at the pictures again for the millionth time. He opened the curtains and looked at the buildings that were untouched by the bombs. The blackbirds were everywhere. They were on every rooftop, every tree and the sky was almost black from them. He then looked into the heavens, thinking that maybe he was going to see God or something. Instead, he heard a voice.

"Nick."

He spun around, but no one was there.

"Julie can help. And there is a child."

"A child?"

"There is a small child who needs someone. She and Julie can help."

"A small child. Where can I find her?"

"You'll find her. Not to worry."

He glanced out the window and once again saw an angel. It was his angel. The one in his pictures.

"She's a guardian angel, Nick, but be careful, she cannot protect you from everything, but she can help."

"Why me? Why have I been chosen for this assignment?"

"Because you asked."

"Oh yeah."

The angel disappeared. The voice went away.

Nick shook his head and paced the room. He almost doubted his own sanity.

Chapter Five

Julie unwrapped the bandages from the tiny child's head. It had sustained much damage but was healing nicely.

"I'm lucky to be alive," the small child told her nurse.

"I know you are."

"My mommy, daddy and brothers are all dead. I miss them. I want my mommy," her big brown eyes in tears.

Julie held her in her arms. She too began to weep. It wasn't fair. Why was all of this happening? It didn't seem fair. "You're very special, Alexis. We'll try hard to find you a new home."

Alexis was one of numerous children who'd ended up on the orphan's list in recent years due to the violence. They'd been unable to locate other family members who could take her. She was a cute, adorable little girl. Julie had become attached to her in the four months she'd been in the hospital. She wanted to take her home.

She glanced at her watch. The sexy patient had been on her mind all day and she now had time to help him with a shower.

Grabbing a wheel chair, she spun it around, sat in it, and pushed herself down the crowded hall. The hospital was full as usual. People reached and laughed at her as she passed in the chair. The long days were taking their toll. The minute ride in a wheel chair was a simple break. A great stress reliever.

Her patient was on the bed chewing his fingers.

"Good afternoon," she greeted him politely.

"Hi." His voice was raspy.

"What happened to your voice?"

"Don't know. It just went on me, just now."

"Is it sore?"

"A little."

"I'll get the doctor to look at it. Ready for your shower?"

His eyes widened. "Yes. Thank you. That would be great."

He gathered his shaving gear and pulled the fishhook out of his soap. He then grabbed his pictures. If someone stole his pack, he would at least have a set of pictures.

"Not going to let them out of sight?"

"I don't need that chair."

"Sit," she commanded.

He did as told.

She wheeled him out the door and down to the shower area. It was a large, musky room.

"Can you undress yourself?"

"I think so." His voice only a whisper.

She watched as he pulled his shirt over his head revealing strong, broad, beautiful shoulders.

"You can shower sitting down in the chair if you like."

"No. I'll be okay." He removed his pants, leaving just his underwear.

Julie watched his every move. He was incredibly sexy, with slim, strong legs and a beautiful butt.

He turned on the water.

She watched it pulsating on his flesh. "You okay?" She wanted to climb in with him.

"This feels great. Soap never felt so good."

Julie wrapped a towel around him and pulled it tight. He was even more handsome now that the scum was gone.

"Feel better?"

"Much."

"Could I have a kiss?" he asked and looked up at her, a silly grin on his face.

Julie laughed. She wanted to kiss him all right. She wanted to feel his arms around her.

"Sure." She gave him a peck on the cheek.

"That wasn't much of a kiss."

"Well, it'll have to do." She massaged his shoulders gently.

"How's your throat?"

"Feels like laryngitis."

Nick dropped a coin in the slot and stuck his fingers in 0. It'd been a long time since he'd used a rotary dial. It reminded him of his childhood.

He asked the operator to place a collect call to Vancouver. They were eight hours behind. Jack should be sitting at his desk setting up assignments.

The phone rang twice. His secretary put him through. "Nick, how are you?"

The familiar sound of his voice helped him relax.

"Hi, Jack." He could barely talk.

"What happened to your voice?"

"Don't know. I quit smoking."

"You quit smoking. Well, that would do it. Are you okay? I've been really worried about you. They've dropped another bunch of bombs over there. Glad to hear you're still alive."

"Thanks." Jack was always so brutally honest.

"Where are you?"

"Oh, I'm still here. And...I think I might be on to something."

"Like what? I think you should come home while you still can."

"What do you know about angels, doves and peace?" His voice barely audible.

"Pardon me? That's a strange question."

"Doves and angels. What do you know about them?"

The line was silent for a minute. "I did a piece on angels while in university. Doves are little white birds."

"Really?" Nick was sarcastic.

"Angels carrying messages of hope and peace have appeared in the Bible and other religious writing for more than two-thousand years. Why?"

"Just wondering."

"Stories of angels have appeared even before the Bible but it was not until about the fourth century AD that angels were presented as having wings. The wavy hair, halos, and white robes came two centuries later. During the fourteenth century, in the early Renaissance, artists began giving angels feminine and childlike features."

"Hold it." Nick grabbed the little tape recorder from his pocket and held it to the phone.

"Say that again."

"Nick what are you doing?"

"Just repeat what you just said."

"I'm expecting blood, bombs and gore. You're giving me doves and angels?"

"Humor me."

Jack laughed. He repeated what he'd said. "Images of young, rose-cheeked angels become popular symbols of hope during the Victorian era. Christ's birth and the traditions that grew out of Victorian Yuletide celebrations have given these winged creatures a very special place in today's Christmas." He paused to catch his breath. "Noah released a single white dove from the ark. Celebrations and ceremonies around the world have released many doves as a symbol of hope, peace, faith and everlasting love."

The line went silent.

"You still there, Nick?"

"Yes. I'm thinking. It hurts to talk, but I need to stay longer. I'm in the hospital right now."

"The hospital?"

"Yeah, there's a cute nurse here."

Jack chuckled. "Are you staying because of the cute nurse or are you sick?"

"I'm working."

"It sounds like it."

"I really can't leave right now. I need another week."

"Another week. Why? Can't you travel?"

"No. It's not that."

"Well, it's not like you're down in Jamaican soaking up the hot sun."

"No kidding. I'll get back to you later."

"Yes. You take care. Oh, and Samantha called looking for you the other day. Your cell is off or something."

"Battery's dead."

"Stay in one piece. I need you."

"Thanks." He hung up the phone.

"I don't see anything," the doctor said, looking into his throat. "Do you want some lozenges?"

"Maybe later." Nick wasn't big on doctor's medicine. He'd always cured everything with a good stiff drink.

"How are you feeling? I mean, besides your throat?"

"Okay. A bit better."

"Okay enough to be discharged?"

Nick pondered the thought. "Maybe tomorrow." That would give him another day's rest.

"Okay. I'll sign the form." The doctor left the room.

He looked over at Julie sitting on the edge of his bed. "I have a spare room in my apartment. It isn't much, but it's something."

"A room?"

"Yes, if you are looking for a place to stay, that is."

"Oh, I need a place to stay alright. Is it quiet?"

"Somewhat. It's on the outskirts of town. There's a nice woodsy area out back."

"Woods."

"Yes. Do you like woods?"

Nick thought back to the other night. He wasn't sure he wanted to see woods ever again."

"I have power and water again. They restored everything last week."

"Are you sure I won't be in your way?"

"No. No. Not at all. It would be nice to have company."

"Okay then, it's settled. Tomorrow we go to your place."

Her smile was sincere and genuine. She was like sunshine on a cloudy day.

Nick slept well. First thing in the morning he was out in the hall with his camera. In the next room he found a nurse tending to an injured leg. He gently knocked, then entered the ward of six men. Most were awake.

The nurse looked at him and smiled.

"I'm a reporter from the *Tribute*. It's a Canadian magazine. I was wondering if I could do some interviews." He held up his identification.

"I know who you are. Tell your army boys to quit dropping bombs."

"I don't have much to do with that. And it's the Air Force that's dropping the bombs. The Army boys are peacekeepers." Nick's voice was harsh and sore.

"Well, whoever it is, just tell them to stop. Look at these people. Come here and look at this guy. He was in a bunker that was hit. Most of his friends have died."

Nick held his hand in the air. "I'm just here to interview and take pictures. I have no control over the war but I can write something if you like."

"Just get them to stop."

"Do you think it's okay for people to be slaughtering and executing other humans?"

The nurse was silent.

"The bombs stopped the Japanese and Hitler. Unfortunately it's the only language mad men like Milosevic understand."

The nurse shook her head and went back to work. "Go ahead," she said. "Talk to who ever you want. I don't care."

He was going to anyway. He didn't need her permission, but now that he had it, he felt better. "Can you interpret what they are saying?"

"Only if you promise to stop the war."

"I'll do my best."

The stories were all the same. Milosevic had responded to the bombings by sending out death squads. He herded tens of thousands of Kosovar Albanians into buses and trains, driving them across the mountainous border into the neighboring Balkan countries. Nick remembers the pilots being under pressure to help slow down the mobility of the Serb forces on the ground. That was why the decision to start bombing had happened.

He looked at their injuries, the pain etched on their faces. He thought about Milosevic sitting in his office, reading his morning paper, sipping on coffee.

"Are you going to eat that?" he asked one guy, pointing to his breakfast tray.

"Just the eggs. Go ahead, have the toast."

Nick gladly accepted and devoured the soggy piece of bread. He interviewed several more people. Most of them were from the Kosovo Liberation Army. They weren't saying much.

Nick left the room.

He went to a few more rooms before arriving in the children's wing. Here he really felt the magnitude of grief. The children's stories were of innocence, pain, and sorrow. Stories that would rock the hearts of most North Americans would they dare to listen.

Then he saw her, her hastily braided hair, big sad eyes and gracious smile.

"What's your name?"

"Alexis."

"That's a pretty name." He knelt beside her wheelchair.

"What's wrong with your voice?"

"I don't know."

"Maybe you talk too much."

Nick laughed. "Maybe. Can I take your picture?"

"Of me? You want to take my picture?" She squealed with delight. "Yes. Take my picture."

Nick backed up and aimed the camera. He saw the angel. It was the same angel as his pictures. She was behind and above Alexis. He looked away from the camera but didn't see her. Then when he looked in to the camera again, she was there. She had wavy hair and wings but no halo.

"Talk to me," Nick said.

"What do you want me to say?" Alexis asked. She flashed her precious smile.

"Not you. Her." He pointed at the angel, almost shouting.

Alexis smiled again.

The nurses were watching. "Did you see that?" he asked them.

"What?"

"Oh, never mind." He didn't want to be thought of as a lunatic.

Nick took several shots from different angles. He captured the angel in all of them. He then went over to Alexis, knelt by her side and whispered: "Do you ever hear voices? Like when no one is around, do you ever hear anything?"

"Sometimes I do."

"Me too."

"I see my angel in here sometimes," she whispered. Her face was one of total innocence.

"Your angel?"

"Yes. Is she real? Do you see her?"

Nick was relieved to hear her words. "Yes, honey. The angel is real."

Nick placed his pack in the back of Julie's car, climbed into the passenger's seat. "I need to get some groceries."

"We can do that tomorrow. I have lots for now. Tomorrow is my day off."

News of her day off excited Nick.

"Is your voice any better? Does it hurt?"

"A little. It's because I quit smoking."

Julie laughed. "You think that did it?"

They drove through a neighborhood, passing a large area of destruction.

"What happened here?"

"One of NATO's errors. Ten people died, including three little children."

Her words caused a sinking feeling in the pit of his stomach.

On the outskirts of town, they drove past the Canadian Army base. He was happy to see the Canadian Flag flapping in the gentle breeze. He wanted to visit.

Julie lived in the back of a large older house. It was a small but quaint little apartment. A little back deck opened onto an overgrown yard filled with tall grass. Behind the woods were mountains.

"This is nice, Julie. Really nice."

"It's quiet. Or it was—quiet. I'll make some supper. Do you want a shower?"

"Do I need one?" He smelt his armpits. He should wash his clothes.

"You smell okay, but you were in the hospital. Who knows what you may have picked up."

She had a point. He thought about asking for help showering. He changed his mind.

The pulsation of the water beat on his back, tenderized his aching muscles. The shower made him feel like a new person. When he emerged from the bathroom, the aroma of home cooking reminded him of Samantha. She loved to cook for him He often thought she'd made it her life's ambition.

Nick roamed the little living room. It was small but comfortable. A small china stand sat in the corner. On it were ornaments and figurines. Nick was drawn to it. Sitting in the center shelf was one of Noah's Ark, the flood that supposedly destroyed the world by a forty day rain fall.

"Do you believe there was a Noah's Ark?"

"I don't think the flood was as big as people think. I think it only wiped out Palestine. There has always been so much violence there. Long historical hatred."

He admired the little dove on the bow. It had an olive leaf. "And after forty days of rain, Noah released a raven, which never returned. Then he released a dove, which returned with an olive leaf. Then after seven days he released the dove again and it didn't return, indicating land was near. When Noah finally left the Ark, God, who caused a rainbow as a sign of his covenant that another flood will not occur again, blessed him. A covenant is a promise."

"Do you know the Bible well?"

"Not really. I tried to read it a few times. There is too much violence in it. Besides, I don't believe half of it. Some stuff might be right on."

Nick was mesmerized and fascinated with the delicately crafted figurine. He picked it up and flipped it over. It was made in China.

There was a blue blouse hanging on the door handle.

Nick removed it, arranged it on the couch, placed the Ark in the center and photographed it.

Julie returned to the room. "What are you doing? That's my best blouse." She was almost hysterical.

"Sorry, I wasn't thinking. It's for something I'm working on. I'll iron it for you, I promise." He takes a couple more shots then aimed the camera at her in her robe and wet hair.

"Could you maybe wait until I put some clothes on?"

Nick chuckled. "Sure, I can do that." His voice a laryngitis mess. "Is there some place I can plug my phone in? I need to recharge the batteries."

They dinned in candlelight with red wine. That too reminded him of Samantha.

"How long will you be staying in Kosovo?"

"I'm not sure. I'm not leaving until I have enough information." He wanted to tell her about the vision, the voices, the harps, the angels, and all that stuff, but he wasn't sure she would believe him. The voice said Julie could help but how? Maybe she was helping by letting him stay with her.

By the time they opened a third bottle of wine, they were both inebriated. They talked about everything and anything except Nick's work and what was happening to the ravished country.

Sitting beside each other on the couch, soft music playing, Nick wrapped his arms around her and kissed her. The passion quickly grew and within moments they were both nude. Nick fondled her tiny breasts. Julie played with his limp penis. For some reason he was unable to get a boner.

"I'm sorry. It must be the wine."

"It's okay. We don't know each other very well."

Nick wasn't sure if it was the wine or not. He didn't understand. He'd never had this problem with Samantha. In fact, it was always the opposite, and they could never get enough of each other.

"Were things any different when this area was the greater Yugoslavia?"

Julie laughed. "Yeah right. This area has always been known for bitter hostility, prolonged feuding and tribal vendettas. There are literally thousands of different ethnic groups who are antagonistic toward one another. It's like it's their inborn right to hate."

Nick absorbed her words.

"Actually we had some peace for twenty or thirty years. Before Milosevic came to power. Fifty years ago it was the Albanians who were attacking the Serbs. Now it's the other way around. About twenty years ago rioting Albanians were stoning and beating outnumbered Serbs. It was the Albanian men who were raping the Serbian women. So the Serbs created a state controlled militia that went around shooting Albanians, including kids making victory signs. People would go into other people's houses and shoot each other. The Yugoslav ideal was supposed to be that contentious people can all live together. Everyone is Yugoslav, but underneath they are something else. Twenty-four-million people, three major religions, and twenty-four ethnic groups. The economy got bad with the increase in population. Our standard of living sunk to the mid-sixties. Each ethnic group blames the other. Milosevic pushed his way to power on one issue—persecution of Albanians in Kosovo. Kosovo, the sacred heart of medieval Serbia."

The way it looked to Nick was it was just ethnic groups hating each other. "Well, hopefully they'll get things under control soon. If they can get Milosevic out of power, they can get a sane government in its place. He's the current problem. His little round head and piggy eyes."

"Many people spent time in prison for simply airing their views. Our refugee problem is compounded by the fact that all the international relief workers left when NATO starting bombing. Our badly needed supplies are all locked down."

"That sucks."

"Did you hear about the phenomenon called Medjugorje?"

"No."

"On June 24 1981, six teenagers came in from the hills near Sarajevo. They said they saw the Virgin Mary. She weeps there daily, crying she wants peace. It's a popular tourist attraction in the town of Mostar up on a mountain point.

"Sounds interesting." Nick was glad she'd told him that. Maybe this spiritual thing he was experiencing had more to it than he realized.

They lay on the carpet in front of the couch. A loud bang roared from outside.

Startled, Nick jumped and ran to the window. Seeing nothing, he slowly opened the door and peeked out. He decided the coast was clear and went to the end of the sidewalk.

Julie followed.

"There's a house on fire down there."

"Looks like they blew up another one?"

"Who?"

"Who knows? Each side blames the other for everything. Albanians live there. Maybe it's the Kosovo Liberation Army. They are a militia group that formed in 1992 to protect themselves against the aggression of Serb police. The Serbs call them terrorists. There are about ten-thousand of them now."

People were running in the streets. A large crowd quickly gathered. "Should we go join them?" Nick wondered.

"No thanks. I've done my humanitarian chores for the day. Enough people know I'm here if they need me. There's a house of young missionaries from the United States living down there. They're really helpful at times like this."

They returned to the comfort of her little home. A home was supposed to be a safe haven. Walls that were meant to keep the love in and the bad out. Here, there was no safe haven. It must be stressful to live with that type of constant animosity toward each other.

In his drunken stupor, Nick laid down on the floor. He thought about how close the explosion was to them. They could die at any minute in this Hell on earth.

Nick woke up and looked around. He was still on the floor. There was a warm blanket over him.

He didn't see nor hear Julie. He was stiff, sore and had a headache. He remembered the fourth bottle of wine and fell back onto the hard floor. What was happening to him? His voice was gone. His dick was limp. He reached into his crotch to check that it was still there. He found it, but it was small and shriveled. He barley recognized it.

He could hear the blackbirds outside. He looked at the kitchen window. They were out there, flying around, squawking.

His cell phone rang, causing him to jump. Talk about jittery. He wondered who was trying to track him down. Very few people had his number. He clicked it on. "Nick here."

"Nick. Hi. It's Samantha. What's wrong with your voice?" He could barely hear her through the static.

"Don't know. It just went. I quit smoking."

"You did. Wow! That's great! Congratulations."

"Thanks."

"So that made your voice go?"

"I think so."

"Where are you?"

"Kosovo."

"Oh, you're still there?"

"You got it."

"That's Bosnia, right?"

"No, Bosnia is to the northwest of here. Bosnia is a country in the Balklan Peninsula. Kosovo is a province of Yugoslavia, or something like that. They keep changing the boundaries."

75

"You've been there for weeks now." Her voice was full of disappointment.

She was probably upset that he wasn't going to lay her tonight.

"Why are you still there? What's taking so long?"

"I'm covering the war."

"Well, it better be worth it. Things are pretty insane. I've been watching it on the news. They're dropping bombs all over the place."

"No kidding." His voice came back.

"That sounds better. How long has it been gone?"

"Couple of days."

"Well see what talking to me can do for it."

She had a point.

"I was calling to invite you over for dinner. I really need to talk to you about something."

The last time she'd said that, she'd seduced him.

"I don't know, Sam. It'll just stir up all those emotions again. Besides, I'm too far away." His voice was back to normal.

"When are you coming back?"

"I'm not sure. I'm sort of onto something."

"I really miss you, Nick. Just come over some night when you get back. We'll have a non-emotional, non-committal dinner. Come on, you have to eat anyway."

"Maybe I'll call you when I get back. You really should move on with your life. You know I'm not what you need." She wanted commitment and that thought was too much for him to handle. He did love her, but he loved his freedom more. He could never be the person she needed.

"It's hard when you're in love."

He wished she wouldn't use words like that. It made it even harder to let her go. "Maybe I'll call you when I get back, I'm not making any promises."

"Where are you?"

"I told you, Kosovo."

"I know, but where are you staying?"

"At a friend's."

"Oh. Male or female?"

He knew she was going to ask. He paused for a second and finally said, "female."

He could sense the tension through the line, even from half way around the world. He marveled at the wonders of technology.

"Oh. That's nice." Her monotone took a downward spiral.

"It isn't what you think, Sam. She's helping me out. I got into a little bit of trouble."

"What kind of trouble?"

He didn't want to get into it again. "I'll tell you when I get back. It's a type of Hell over here."

"I'll look forward to it."

"To what?"

"To you coming for dinner and telling me all about it."

Nick ate his words. She would probably wait for him for forever. That thought made him feel guilty. He shouldn't feel guilty, it wasn't his fault.

"Oh, and Nick, I love you."

"I know you do. Bye." He couldn't tell her what she wanted and needed to hear.

He fell onto the couch and stretched out.

Julie came out of her room. "Good morning."

"Hi."

"Your voice is back."

"Yes."

"You had a phone call?"

"Friend from back home checking up on me."

"I hope you told them you were in good hands." She made coffee.

Nick rubbed the throbbing at the back of his neck. "I did."

"Today's my day off. What do you want to do?"

He thought for a moment. What he really wanted to do was go home and smoke a big fat joint in his living room and vegetate.

"Do you think maybe we could go to that Canadian Army base we passed yesterday? I'd like to try and get in there and do some interviews."

"We can try." He detected a hint of hesitation in her voice.

He flipped on the TV. They'd dropped more bombs near Belgrade, taking out the cities TV station, killing several journalists and support staff. They also hit a military vehicle compound and a bridge.

"Nick. Can I ask you something?"

"Sure."

"You said you have been in Kosovo for two weeks now, right?"

"That's right."

"Are you trying to get the entire story of the war? Like from beginning to end, or what exactly is it you are writing about?"

He thought carefully, weighing each word. He was going to risk the chance she would think him to be a psychopathic lunatic. Who's ever going to believe his story? He felt like a lunatic anyway, so what the heck.

"Sit down." He patted the couch. He didn't know where to start. It was so bizarre. He started at the beginning. He told her about being in the ancient village of Devin, inside the store. Rebel troops had come in with their guns and hatchets. They lined everyone up in a drainage ditch. Then in execution style, shot and slaughtered them. The shopkeeper took off out back. He had taken a few pictures through the window.

He continued with the rest of the story. He hesitated when he got to the part about praying to God while in the bush. He wasn't sure if he should continue, but decided he would.

He took a sip of coffee. It was the worst coffee he'd ever tasted.

He continued talking. Again he hesitated when he got to the part about the sunrise. "And the sky turned the most incredible colors. I heard harps playing and angels singing. Doves and angels were flying everywhere."

Julie gave him a funny look.

Not her too. Another non-believer. "Come on, Julie, you saw the pictures. I need you with me on this. And that isn't it. While I was in the hospital I spoke to the angel who told me you and a small child could help."

"Really?"

"Yes, and when I photographed Alexis I saw the angel again. Do you know little Alexis from the children's wing?"

"Oh, I know her all right. She's really cute. Her family's home was hit with a grenade or something."

"She told me she'd spoken with the angel. The one that's in all of the pictures."

He went to his pack and grabbed the pictures. "Take a close look at these, the same angel is in all of them."

As she glanced through them, Nick gave her more details. The part about the politicians and the United Nations baffled him the most. What was he supposed to do with this information?

Julie was stunned. She paced the living room. "Is this all true? You aren't making it up?"

"You saw the pictures. Everyone saw the doves."

"Yes, but only you saw angels."

"Anyway, it doesn't matter. I have to do something with all this. I don't know what. Are you with me or not? Are you going to help me or not?"

She glanced at him. He was sure she had love in her eyes. "Of course." She sat down beside him and patted his shoulder. "Of course, I will help you any way I can. I don't know how, but yes, I will help."

"Just believe in me. Just believe that what I'm telling you is the truth."

"Okay, I believe you. You have to admit though, it all does sound pretty strange. But, Nick, if you can figure out how to stop the fighting…think about it, it's been going on since the beginning of time. How on God's earth are you going to get them all to stop fighting?"

"Did you know that the Holocaust, in which more than six-million Jews died, was basically legal?"

"Eh?"

"You heard me. The right of nations come first over the laws of the United Nations."

"So they need to switch things around."

"That's right. They need to make sure that anyone, including heads of state or high-ranking generals, who commit humanitarian crimes is charged. Maybe at the Hague, maybe elsewhere."

"Hague, what's that?"

"It's a city, a seat of government of the Netherlands and capital of South Holland province. The Supreme Court of the Netherlands and the States-General parliament are located there. It's also the site of most foreign embassies. And the city is home to the International Court of Justice, a United Nations agency that was established in 1993 to prosecute breaches of the 1949 Geneva Convention, violations of the laws or customs of war, genocide and crimes against humanity."

"How do you know all of that?"

"I'm a reporter. It's my job."

Nick watched Julie pace the living room. Her petite and perfectly curvy body dazzled him. He didn't understand what had happened with his inability to perform. He figured it was the wine.

"How are you going to do it, Nick?"

"Do what?"

"The United Nations thing. Are you just going to write a story and hope some power head reads it?"

Nick thought about the power of the media. He went to the kitchen and made an ice pack for his head then lay down.

Julie picked up a King James version of the Bible. "Listen to this," she read. "Likewise, I say to you, there is joy in the presence of the angels of God over one sinner that repenteth. That's Luke 15, paragraph 10."

"What does repenteth mean?" Nick asked. He thought he knew, but wanted to be sure.

"Repent means to turn from sin or feel regret, sorrowful…you know."

"Sorry, I'm not very religious. I believe in God. I know for a fact he exists, but I've never read the Bible, nor attended much Church."

"Why not?"

"I don't know, just never got around to it I guess. The Catholic religion and confession thing is stupid if you ask me." He thought about his deep Irish Catholic roots.

"Why do you say that?"

"Gives you permission to be an asshole."

Julie laughed. "I hate that crucifix that they hang all over the place."

Julie was flipping through the book, picking out pages. "God is our refuge and strength, a very present help in trouble. Palm, 46, paragraph 1."

"You can say that again. He sure works in mysterious ways."

"Blessed are the peacemakers, for they shall be called the children of God. Matthew 5, paragraph 9."

"Hold on, Let me get my tape recorder." He hobbled over to his equipment. His head still throbbing.

"The peacekeepers have sure helped us out." She was pacing the room with the book in her hands.

"Thou shalt love thy neighbor as thyself."

"Pretty much says it all." He watched her gracefully move around the room.

"This is my commandment, that yea love one another as I have loved you. John 15, paragraph 12."

"You're really hitting the nail on the head."

Julie closed the Bible and threw it on the chair. She sat down beside Nick. "Every law of God is being broken here in Kosovo. Thou shalt love thy neighbor. You call this love?"

Nick gazed deep into her brown eyes. They looked pained.

"No, this isn't love, it's the furthest thing from it. This is Hell. This is the kind of Hell only the devil wishes for. This is not God's wish. He would not wish for this type of thing, I'm sure."

Julie buried her face in her hands.

Nick rubbed her back. "Things will get better, you'll see. Things have to improve. The bombs have worked before. They worked with Hitler, they worked in Iraq, and they will stop him."

"Sure after they have destroyed our cities and killed thousands of innocent people, then, and maybe only then it will all stop."

"I know, it comes with a heavy price, but right now there's no other way. As long as there are madmen running countries, there's no other way." He was trying to comfort her badgered soul. He was so appreciating being Canadian. He thought about how, as a child and teenager, he'd taken everything for granted. He'd been raised on a farm, far removed from any violence, surrounded with fresh air, wildlife, cow manure and fence posts. Sure, he'd worked hard as a child on the farm, but life had been simple and uncomplicated. Here, life for the youth is nothing but fear. It didn't seem fair. There had to be a better way to get all tyrannical governments around the world out of power. Human rights for everyone. How else could they do it without using force? When diplomatic talks fail with evil dictators, how do you get them out of power without the use of force? Sanctions rarely if ever work. Madmen know no limits, a well know history lesson from the terror days of the Japanese and Hitler.

He embraced her.

She turned and kissed him gently on the lips. "Thanks."

"For what?"

"For being here. For caring. For risking your life to tell our story."

He wanted to make love with her. He didn't understand. She'd given him a boner at the hospital, but here he was impotent. Maybe he was getting old, maybe the stress was taking a toll.

"Can I ask about your boyfriend?"

"Yes. He was a University student and part of an activist union they'd formed. They were quickly becoming a leading voice in the opposition of Milosevic's regime, were extremely organized and the media loved them. One weekend they were holding a demonstration on a sport's field down by the Sava River below Belgrade's old fort. They started doing mock military training, you know karate lessons and stuff like that. The police showed up. When the police asked them what they were doing, they said they were exercising. The police didn't like the humor and tried to arrest them. Violence broke out and Roeg was shot, along with others. It was senseless. Totally senseless." The tears tumbled over her cheeks.

Tears formed in Nick's eyes. He embraced her and held her tight. It was a sad story, but he was happy to hear that the youth were aware that Milosevic needed to be over thrown.

Their moment of embrace was interrupted by Nick's cell phone ringing. He switched it on and said hello.

"Hey Nick. Jack here. They finally have the satellite hooked up."

"What?"

"The satellite. I haven't been able to reach you on your phone because the satellites were knocked out."

"No, my batteries were dead."

"Anyway, I need you to come home. I have something more important for you to do?"

He couldn't believe what he was hearing. "What could be more important than this?"

"Microsoft. They're suing bill Gates for breaking anti-trust laws. This is big, Nick. Really big."

His words made his heart sink. He didn't give a shit about Microsoft. "I can't leave, Jack, I'm in too deep."

"Deep in a story or deep in love? Kosovo is all over the TV; it's old news, Nick. It's just the same story over and over again. I really need you on this Microsoft thing."

The phone was silent. "No, I can't." He almost felt like decking him one. Old news. How dare he refer to what was going on as old news?

"You can't or *won't*. Where are you anyway?"

"Staying with a friend."

"Female. Cute nurse?"

"Yes."

"I knew it. Nick, this isn't some paid romantic holiday you know. Now get on the next plane or you're officially off the payroll."

Nick chuckled. Paid romantic holiday in Kosovo. Whatever. "Don't do that."

"I have no choice. I have to answer to the magazine. I have bosses. They have bosses. You aren't making any sense. So get your buns home now. Hear me. Now."

"I can't, Jack. I'm on to something. I can't explain. Besides I *want* to do this." He wondered if he would believe him if he told him about his night in the bush. Probably not.

"Are you in trouble?"

"Not at the moment."

"How long do you need?"

"I don't know."

"One more week and that's it. Nick, you were supposed to be gone for the weekend. You're into your third week now. One more week and that's it."

"Fine."

"Good luck with whatever it is you are up to. This better be good. You better not be fucking the dog over there."

He really had a way with words. He looked at Julie. "Do you own a dog?"

"No. Why?"

"I just don't want you to burn out, Nick. I need you. I've seen people fry in places like that. Some never return to normal."

"Thanks for your concern, Jack. I promise, you won't be sorry. And if you are, I'll resign."

"Ughh, don't do that. Stay in touch, Nicky ole boy."

"Sure, boss. Talk to you later." He hung up and glanced at Julie. "My boss. He wants me home to cover the Microsoft story."

"What's that?"

"A giant software company. You know what a computer is, right."

"Yes."

"Well, Microsoft designs user friendly software. Ninety-five percent of people with computers use it."

"And…"

"And, well, you know, when someone has something really good, someone else always wants to sabotage them. There's a big lawsuit saying they violated anti trust laws."

"Which are?"

"Laws designed to protect the consumer. Laws to prevent a large corporation from having a monopoly, thus driving up unfair prices."

"Did he break them?"

"Well, it's complicated. A lawyer I spoke to about it told me this story. Bill Gates bought the Windows operating system from a neighbor for $200."

"Wow."

"The neighbor eventually killed himself. Anyway, so Gates tried to sell the program to International Business Machines where he was working at the time. They declined because they thought they had a better operating system, so Bill Gates does it on his own, calling it Microsoft. He made lots of deals with the government who let him eat up all the smaller software companies in exchange for high tech software. He thinks the lawsuit may be just for show."

"They let him take over the companies?"

"Hostile takeover. They set themselves up on the stock market and Microsoft offered them more than the shares were worth."

"Sounds like he invented the best program then received a lawsuit for it."

"He doesn't invent them, he buys them."

"So he's the engineer behind everything. Right?"

"He pays more for stock than they're worth."

"But if your company is on the stock market and someone offers you more than your company is worth you don't *have* to sell."

Nick laughed. She had a point. "Basically. Stupid, aye. Jack wants me to cover the story. It could drag on for years."

"You said no."

"Of course, this is more important."

"Thanks, Nick, for everything. I mean it."

"I haven't done anything."

"You're giving me a sense of security."

The words made him shiver. He desperately needed his emotional freedom right now. Julie was in a vulnerable state. He didn't want to hurt her like he had Samantha. "You are a very beautiful person, Julie, but you know I can't stay forever. Please don't get emotionally involved with me."

Julie gazed into his eyes. Her soul was loving and caring. "I respect your honesty."

Nick walked over to the large glass door in the kitchen and stared out the window. The trees were a beautiful mix of oak, maple, elm, pine, and fir, much like most of the trees he knew from back home. The grass in her back yard was long and unkept with weeds everywhere. "Do you ever mow your lawn?"

"No. Can't be bothered. Besides, I don't own a lawnmower."

It was a rustic yard. He mellowed at the view. He loved the outdoors, preferring the bush to the city.

"Why didn't you go to Europe with your parents?"

"I was in love with Roeg. My mother met my father in Belgrade when she was working at the embassy. This is my home. I've been here all of my life. Besides, these people need help."

She was a humanitarian. Full of compassion. True humanitarians risk life and limb for others. If there were more people like her, the world would be a better place.

He rubbed his forehead and turned to look at her.

She was sitting in the rocking chair, rocking back and forth, watching him. Watching his every move.

"Are there any land minds out back?"

"I don't think so."

Chapter Six

The Canadian flag proudly flapped in the wind. Nick saluted it as they drove past.

"I'm with the *Tribute*." Nick flashed his pass to the guard at the makeshift Army base.

He looked at his identification and checked his clipboard. "I know that magazine. It's been around for years. Do you have an appointment with someone?"

Nick looked at his rifle. It looked heavy. "No, I'm doing a story and was wondering if I could interview some people. Like you, how about you?"

"Me?" He smiled and checked out the camera in his lap. "I have to check your pack."

"Sure. Go ahead. You'll find a tape recorder, a laptop, film, you know, the usual press stuff."

The private opened the door, unzipped the bag and peered inside. He did it back up.

"And your driver? Who's she?"

Julie handed him her I.D. "Ethnic Albanian, born and raised right here in Pristina." She had a beautiful smile.

Nick looked at her. "You're Albanian. I thought you were Serb. You work in a Serb hospital."

"Doesn't matter. The sick and injured need help. These people are my neighbors."

She *really* was a humanitarian.

The private checked the identification with her face. "Let me get the captain. He'll probably want you to have an escort." He went to his Jeep and picked up the headset.

Nick and Julie looked over to the jungle of green tents, neatly in rows. At one door sat a large peanut butter jar containing dried flowers. Nick smiled. He zoomed in on it and snapped a few shots. He then pointed his camera over to the private. Low and behold, there was his little angel. "Look into this camera. Quick." He shoved it into Julie's face.

Julie gave him a weird look and took it. She peered through the lens. "Nice camera."

"Do you see anything strange?" He leaned over and whispered in her ear, "Like an angel?"

"No, Nick, I don't see anything."

"Well look again."

She took one more look. The private returned. Julie handed him back his camera.

"The captain is on his way. Are you the guy they picked up in the bush the other morning?"

"Yes. Did you hear about that?"

"The captain was wondering. What are you writing about?"

Nick analyzed every hair on his face. "It's about peace. Part two to love and war."

"Really?"

"No." Nick winked at him. "Mind if I take your picture?"

"Sure." He posed at his Jeep.

Nick got his name.

"I'm Captain Black." He shook their hands. "What can I do for you today?"

Nick looked at the stripes on his uniform. "I'm a reporter for the *Tribute*. This is my friend Julie, she's a local."

"Nice to meet you, and…"

"I'm writing a story about the war and was wondering about the role you people are playing. Do you have a few minutes?"

The captain glanced at his watch. "I'm okay for a bit, but I may have to rush off. Go ahead, ask me anything."

"How many troops are there?"

"About twelve-hundred Canadians."

"And what role are you playing?"

"We are here to keep the peace. Just like the title says, peacekeeper."

"And the bombs?"

"That's the Air Force. This is the Army, we're the people on the ground."

"Of course." Nick knew that, he just wanted it on tape.

"And what are your duties?"

"We do patrols, carrying out vehicle checks, confiscate arsenal and ensure camp security for refugees and ourselves. Our goal is to keep the peace."

The Captain gave them a tour of the camp. Pretty basic stuff, tents, tents, and more tents. Nick took tons of pictures, seeing his angel in most.

They came to the end of the row. Then he smelled it. Oh, the sweet aroma coming from the second last tent.

The captain had a disapproving look on his face. He turned to lead them in the opposite direction. "Come back this way, there's nothing down here."

"Do you smell that?" Nick asked. A silly grin on his face.

The Captain looked at him. "I'll deal with it when you leave. Please, we don't need scandal."

"Well, I've already smelt it. Please, I just want to talk to them."

"No, I don't think it's a good idea."

"Come on. These guys are Canadian. I'm Canadian. They aren't doing anything really serious except that it's illegal. We used to grow it on the farm when we were teens."

The captain looked at him.

"My mother never knew, of course."

He grinned. "It stays out of the press."

"I promise. Boy Scout honor." He saluted him with two fingers.

"I have to reprimand them."

"Whatever." Nick walked toward the tent, pulled back the flap, and entered. The air was thick with marijuana smoke. Two privates in off duty clothes were sitting on flipped over white pails at a small table playing cards. They were startled by the three figures standing in the doorway. Their eyes bulged. They stood up and saluted the captain.

"I should send you two back home right now."

"What for?"

"Don't play stupid. And this is a member of the press."

The two privates said, "uggg" in unison. "I told you we should've gone outside," one said to the other.

"There was silence for a few moments. " I don't suppose you could leave us alone." Nick asked the captain.

"You got to be kidding."

"Seriously. This is a real interest piece and, yes, it would make one heck of a story, but I'm not here to be vindictive. I would never do anything to undermine the integrity of your services. I have nothing but the utmost of respect for you people and, well, the situation really hits at the heart of the matter. I would really like to interview them in a non-intimidate manner. Consider it an act of benevolence."

"Act of benevolence? Right."

Nick smiled.

"Fine. Five minutes and I'm waiting outside." He looked at the privates. "I'll deal with you two later." He turned and left the tent. The boys saluted.

Julie sat down on the corner of a bed.

The two young privates relaxed a few degrees. They sat back down on their pails.

"I'm from the *Weekly Tribune*. Ever hear of it?"

" I guess we're in some kind of trouble."

"Not with me. Do you guys always smoke pot on base?"

"No. Never. A friend sent me a few joints in the mail. We're on our day off. We were going to air the tent."

"I told you we should've smoked it out behind the tent," his friend said again.

"It's illegal. What happens when you get caught?"

"If the Military Police catch us, it can be pretty stiff. One guy did two years. I'm not sure about the captain. He's a pretty reasonable guy. It just helps us to relax and mellow out. It's far better than getting drunk, which is totally legal. Drink as much whisky as you want, fall down drunk, but hey, don't dare take a puff."

His friend laughed.

"So you just wanted to relax on your day off?" Sounded perfectly normal to Nick.

"You got it."

"And what happens if some type of trouble breaks out, like a rebel troop shows up or something like that and you guys are all stoned up."

They looked at each other. They didn't answer.

"Well?"

"Well, we'll just deal with it."

"Do you like it over here?"

"Oh, it's the thrill of all thrills," one said sarcastically.

"Can you be more specific?"

"Put it this way. I now appreciate the freedom and dignity that we have back home."

"Do you think there is any way the fighting will ever stop?"

The boys laughed. "Maybe when they totally wipe each other out?"

He approached them and spoke silently. "Do you want to sell me one of those joints?"

The boys looked at each other. They had a conversation in French that he didn't understand.

"You guys are bilingual?"

"Oui. We're from Quebec."

One of them stood up and came over to Nick. "We're already in trouble and we don't need to get into any more. We're going to give you the two we have left."

"Great!" Nick squealed.

One of them went over to his pillow, reached down into the bottom of the slip, and pulled out a crumpled Kleenex. He handed it to Nick who shoved it in his pocket.

"You just made my day. How much?"

"It's okay. But be careful. It's killer wheelchair stuff."

"Great." Nick grinned.

Julie stood up. "Nick. What are you doing?"

Nick turned around and put his finger to his lips. "Shhh." He pointed in the direction of the captain as he came back in. Perfect timing. Nick thanked the boys and shook their hands.

Their angelic smiles said it all. They were good looking boys, innocent and tender. He felt for them. He admired and had the utmost respect for them. They were saints in the hatred of life. They were children of God.

"I want to see you two first thing in the morning," the captain told the boys. "And in the meantime, keep your noses clean."

"Yes, sir. That won't be a problem, sir. Supply is finished."

"Glad to hear it."

They saluted the captain.

The three exited the tent.

"What are you going to do to them?" Nick asked.

"I should phone the M.P.'s. They've only been in the service for six months when they were shipped over here. They're young. I don't want to scare them. I'll give them a warning and give them something yucky to do on their day off. Like clean the dumpster."

He was a manager with compassion. The world needed more compassionate people. Nick was happy he wasn't going to be too hard on them. As far as Nick was concerned, it was a harmless bit of weed.

They toured the grounds. It was a true campout. Outhouses, lounges, and cook tents. One guy complained that the tankers had

Coleman stoves and Bisquick while they'd been eating rations. Their master corporal was promising to help them out.

"Anything else you need?" the captain asked.

"No. That just about covers it I think"

He escorted them to the car and shook their hands.

Nick thanked him for his hospitality. They climbed into the car and drove away.

"What did they give you?" Julie asked as she drove through town.

"A couple of joints."

"What!" Julie screamed.

"You don't smoke?"

"No. Get rid of it."

"Okay." Nick put one in his mouth and pushed in her cigarette lighter.

"Not like that. Throw them out."

Nick looked at her. "I can't. I want it. I need it. You don't understand."

"I understand lots. I don't want it in my car."

Nick was silent for a minute. "Okay, I'll leave as soon as we get back to your place."

"You would rather have your weed than be with me?" She freaked.

Nick didn't answer. He sat thinking about the question. He was enjoying Julie's company, but he had work to do and right now he was brain dead. The weed would stimulate the creative juices.

"Well?" she asked again.

"I'll smoke it in the back woods. If the police haul me away, I won't tell them where I'm staying. How's that?"

Julie was silent. It felt like an eternity for her to give him an answer. Finally she said, "Okay."

They stopped at a market. Nick looked at the sickly fruits and vegetables. "Is it always like this? This food isn't very fresh."

"Well, at least there is some here. Lately, there hasn't been much around. In the summer we have beautiful markets."

Nick loaded up with various items.

"Staying a while?" she asked.

"My boss gave me another week."

"Maybe I should take some holidays."

"I have to work. Jack will be expecting a story."

"Oh." Her voice was full of disappointment.

Nick wondered what women saw in him. He was middle aged, going gray, had a spare tire around his waist. His pectoris were turning to mush.

He smoked quarter of a joint. It only took seconds for the effects to hit him. He was catching a good one, roaming in the bush, admiring the trees when a group of children playing war games ran by. They stopped to look, asking him questions in a language he didn't understand. They wanted to touch his camera.

"I only speak English." He showed them the Canadian flag on his identification.

They chattered among themselves.

Nick left the woods, sat on Julie's back step and watched the children. They were no more than twelve years of age and playing war. Children are what they learn.

He picked up his camera, waved it in the air, yelling and signaling for the children to come to him.

They were intrigued.

He asked permission to take their pictures playing their little war game. As they posed in different positions, Nick clicked away. His angel appeared in most pictures. She was fluttering about with her wings, long hair, and flowing gown.

Somewhere in his stoned stupor an idea came to him. It wasn't a new idea, but one that'd been around for a while now. The old childhood role model theory: Children are what they learn. It was an old saying that'd he'd read once. A set of guidelines for parents and child care workers. If a child lives with hostility, he will learn to fight. If a child lives with fairness, he learns justice. If a child lives with security, he learns faith. If a child lives with love, acceptance, and friendship, he learns to find love in the world. They had to start with the children. The North American teachers had caught on to the idea along ago. No guns at school and that included water pistols. Water guns became fireman hoses. No ninja turtles, Power Rangers and no Pokemon going to battle. No games that involved war or violence. No little gray army men. If we wanted a world where there was no violence, we had to start at the bottom. It had to be ingrained into their innocent little minds from birth. If an entire generation around the world was raised at the same time, conditioned to only love each other, be protected, and taught fairness, then the world would live in peace. They needed to be sheltered and protected from the violence coming out of Hollywood and the media. Imagine, an entire generation of them growing up in a loving and peaceful world. It would be sensational. He knew a big problem was sustainable environments. Population explosion occurring in areas not capable of supporting its population base. Creating sustainable environments was a must if they wanted to save planet earth.

It was a fantasy. It was a dream. What if he could somehow make it a reality? If you want to make change, major substantial change, you had to start at the beginning. Take a proactive approach. He thought about how maybe the North American military could move away from defense and become more proactive in war prevention. He laughed. So many tyrants were running countries. That was when it hit him. The politicians. Tyrant governments have to go or there will never be peace on earth.

Julie came onto the back deck and sat beside him. "How was your walk in the bush?"

"Great, I met some kids."

"What? While you were smoking?"

Nick put his hand on her lap. "Calm down, no, they didn't see me smoking. I photographed them. They were playing war."

"Oh, they're always doing that. All the kids in the neighborhood hang around out there. Used to be about fifty of them, but lots have fled the country."

"Why aren't they in school?"

Julie looked at him. "There's a war going on. They bombed both of the schools, the Albanian, and Serb schools. It was right after they bombed the utility plant."

"Who?"

"Each other. They just blow each other up."

"Oh right. Of course, let's cancel school and play war. Brilliant."

Julie rubbed his back. "Can I have a hug?"

Nick stood up and kissed her tenderly on the lips. He embraced her. She was needy and clung tight. He thought about how difficult it must be for her and how strong she is to stay in a place where there was neither security nor stability. She lived in a place where hatred rules the day. Where civil war was daily talk.

"Tell me again why you stay here."

"I don't want to live in a refugee camp. As long as I wear my nursing suit and identification when I go out, I'm fine. Tell me about your girlfriend back home."

"She wants to settle down and I don't. I travel with my work and enjoy my freedom."

He thought about the sex and how great she was in the sack. She could never get enough of him.

"Do you love her?"

Nick thought about the question. Maybe he did. He wasn't sure of anything right now.

He decided not to answer.

It suddenly dawned on him that there was nothing else for him to do in Kosovo. He'd seen enough, taken enough pictures, notes, and tape recordings. What he needed to do was compile the information into a useable format. He needed to get to his workstation.

"I think I'm going to go home. I need my workspace."

The disappointment showed on her face. "What? I thought you were staying a week?"

"I need the lab," he lied. What he really needed was to go home so he could concentrate on what to do with all his bizarre experiences of seeing angels and having voices talk to him."

"Can I go with you?"

Her words surprised him.

"I can get refugee status in North America right now."

Nick jumped up and stood back to look at her. He felt for this young beautiful human being. She'd been thrown into a war she had nothing to do with. A war few wanted.

"You want to go to North America? Or you want to come home with me? What are you asking me, Julie?"

"I don't know."

"What about your parents? Don't you want to be with them?"

"They're in England."

"So. What's wrong with England?"

"Boring."

"Boring?" What could be boring about England? It was a beautiful country.

"I want to see new things. I hear life is really good in Canada."

"We do have a great government. It's cold and rustic for the most part." How could he say anything but yes? "I'll talk to the captain I met and see if he can arrange something." It was the military who were transporting the refugees to North America.

Her face became an expression of excitement. "You're my knight in shining armor."

"I haven't done anything." He picked up the phone and dialed the number he'd jotted down while outside the hospital.

"Captain says there's no problem getting us a flight. There's one leaving on Thursday. Is that okay?" He put the phone on the hook.

"Wow. Great. I'll go to the hospital right now and make arrangements." She was ecstatic. "Do you want to come with me?"

Nick was anxious to jot down an outline for his story. "I'll stay here if you don't mind."

Julie grabbed her keys. "I'll be back in a couple hours."

"Take your time."

She paused at the door. "Thank you so much." She turned and disappeared.

Nick watched her drive away. He turned from the window and noticed her nursing uniform hanging on the doorknob. She'd left the house wearing street clothes.

He went out on the back porch and smoked the rest of the joint. Now he was really stoned. His mind went into overdrive thinking about his message from the spiritual world. "Julie can help, the child can help. The child. He'd forgotten all about little Alexis. If he left Kosovo, he would be leaving the kid behind. Didn't matter. He couldn't figure out how she would be of any help to him anyway. Then there were the politicians and the United Nations. What was he supposed to do with this message?

He set up his laptop on the kitchen table and sat down. He thought about the war because Jack had sent him over here to figure out what all the fighting was about. It was a historical thing. It was just something that'd been going on for so long. It was as though they didn't know anything else. The Serbs would launch rockets into the United Nations Safe zone and blame in on the ethnic Albanians and vice versa. No one would ever take responsibility for his or her actions. It was impossible to separate them because they live in the same neighborhoods, in apartment buildings side by side.

He'd interviewed one Albanian who was friends with a Serb for fifty years. "Those days are over," he'd told him. The Serbs gave the Albanians ten minutes to pack their belongings. He said the next morning they were told they could go home when they returned they found their houses burnt down. His neighbors burnt down his house and told him to go home to Albania that was his country.

There were reports of Serb executions toward Albanians in at least twenty towns and villages. Throughout Kosovo, the cleansing of the provinces 1.8 million Albanians was swift and brutal. Pristina black-masked Serb police dragged Albanians out of their homes. Old warehouses became their wretched homes.

Then there was the Kosovo Liberation Army or the Ushtria Clirimatare E. Kosoves.

Kosovo's President Rugova's position was undermined when the Kosovo Question was left off the agenda at the Dayton Peace talks in

1995. The Albanians wanted their own mini-state. Young Albanians wanted to know why they should behave to nonviolence when the Bosnia Serbs were being rewarded for their brutality. They began to carry out isolated attacks on Serbian police. The violence increased over the years, targeting police stations and military figures.

They functioned as a guerilla movement that was about five-hundred strong at their inception in 1992. They'd now grown to almost 20,000 armed guerillas. They were professionally trained, and most members are former army, state security force, or police. They functioned professionally in the underground. Their members included foreign mercenaries from Albania, Saudi Arabia, Yemen, Afghanistan, Bosnia and Herzegovina and Croatia. There is also believed to be British and German Insurgents. Their primary training camps were in Albania.

Until 1998, they used only light arms, but recently they had been armed with more powerful firearms that included Soviet-designed RPG shoulder-fired anti-tank rocket launchers, mortars, anti-aircraft, machine guns. They also had some weapons from the Second World War, such as PPS-411 rifles and the MP 40. Nick didn't have a clue what all this stuff was.

The KLA had two command centers, one abroad, and one in Pristina. They had well-organized surveillance apparatus and an organized word of mouth messenger service.

Both Rugova and the K.L.A. had insisted upon independence for Kosovo from Serbia. But Serbia rejected this concept, taking the position that Kosovo remained Serbia's internal matter.

It was this armed resistance that gave Milosevic the pretext for his brutal crackdown. In late February 1998, extreme violence broke out between Serbian forces and the KLA. Serbian police then raided villages in Kosovo's Drenica region, a KLA stronghold. They burned homes and killed dozens of ethnic Albanians. Serb police, using tear gas, water cannons, and clubs attacked thousands of Albanian protesters in Pristina.

Thousands of Kosovar Albanians were now displaced from their homes, many fleeing to the hills and forests. The refugees resembled those of the Balkan War in 1912.

Over the summer of 1998, the fighting resulted in the displacement of some 300,000 people. Since then, Milosevic had steadily increased the level of violence against the Albanian majority. He told reporters, "There is no Serb aggression...we are merely protecting ourselves. Besides, the Croats 'cleansed' several hundred thousand Serbs fifty years ago."

The situation escalated in January 1999. By February, the Clinton administration had enforced the Serbian embargo, which forbid U.S. exports of oil, software and other items except food and medicine to the Serbian province, which caused the economy to collapse. The hope of the embargo was to diminish Belgrade regimes ability to continue its campaign of regression. Unfortunately Milosevic benefited from it by controlling a black market.

Sanctions often backfire because they inflict harm on vulnerable civilians. At the time, the Secretary General encouraged the General Assembly and Security Council to consider ways to "render sanction a little less blunt and more effective instrument to reduce the humanitarian cost to civilians." Embargoes usually hurt people at the bottom of the economic population.

On March 19, a peace conference in Paris broke up with Yugoslav delegations refusal to accept a peaceful settlement. By March 24, NATO forces began operations over Yugoslavia with more than thirty-nine days of air strikes.

He thought about a list of reasons he'd once read about why kids bully each other. They do so because they think the world revolves around them. They bully because they feel insecure and bullying makes them feel powerful. They bully because they have low self-confidence and want to be in control. Milosevic must have a low self-esteem and bullying makes him feel powerful. One way to stop the bully is to walk away. A lot of them had done that; they'd fled the country. And they should tell a friend. They did, they told the press. The press told the world, who then came to help. Don't fight back was another tactic. That was suicidal around here. Start a school program. That was it. That was what they needed, a strong humanitarian school program that taught the kids about peace and love. Fighting was wrong. They really did need to love their neighbor. They needed to take a proactive approach to the fighting. He jotted down in his notes: International School Program. He knew it was Article 26 of the Universal Declaration of Human Rights that was adopted in 1948. Everyone has the right to Education. It and shall be free at least in the elementary and fundamental stages. Elementary education is compulsory. Every child learns. It was just another joke for the United Nations. Countries who support child labor were members. There were so many countries who signed the Universal Declaration of Human Rights and who were breaking all the rules. He drew a big dollar sign beside it. How much? How much would it take to set up a school program for every child under twelve? Give them lunch, a uniform, and teach them how to love. How to create more sustainable environments where people are self-sufficient and get a grip on world population control. That was what they need to work toward. And in the meantime, the developing world needed to help the less fortunate. Someone once said that there's enough food grown around the world to feed everyone, but distribution was an issue. It had been two decades ago that he'd heard that. World population had increased by two billion since then and so he wondered if there was still enough food. He thought about the popular Eagle's song, "When we're hungry, love will keep us alive." That was probably why so many kids are born into poverty. What else is there to do when you live in a non-sustainable environment? He wished the Pope would just keep his mouth shut about birth control.

He doesn't know how the time went by, but when he looked at his watch he realized it was late in the evening. Julie said she'd be back in a couple of hours. Already she'd been gone for four.

He fixed something to eat and sat to watch the evening news. Only one station came in. I wasn't very clear. The bombs had knocked out most communications in the country. There was news footage about a group of rebel Serbs who'd set up a roadblock on the southern highway and had taken more Albanians hostage. It never stopped. They never fucking quit. Even the bombs don't stop them.

Chapter Seven

Samantha sat down at her keyboard and stared at the screen. She hated eating alone and would often have lunch with the cursor blinking in front of her.

Nick was on her mind as usual. She needed a hypnotic session to get him out of her system. She thought about giving up on him and finding someone else, but it was hard because she loved him dearly.

She felt a presence behind her, but when she turned no one was there. She wasn't expecting company, but she could have sworn she'd seen an angel standing in the room.

She'd been working on the computer a lot. Perhaps it was having an effect on her eyes. It was probably just a shadow coming in the window from outside.

She opened the door and stood out on the veranda. The heat of the afternoon sun hit her. It was unusually warm for September. It felt more like July. She wondered if global warming was to blame. She heard a voice.

"Nick needs your help."

She spun around, but no one was there. She was losing it. She must be hallucinating.

It gave her an idea for a story line for a new novel. One that she would write someday after she became a famous author. She created a raving lunatic character who was seeing and hearing things.

Nick was getting impatient. It was past nine in the evening and Julie hadn't returned. He called the hospital. It took them an eternity to find someone who spoke English. It then took that person an eternity to call Julie's wing and get the information he needed. The person told him that she'd been there earlier that afternoon and resigned her position. She'd taken Alexis. They were going to Canada.

That was almost seven hours ago. It was only a forty-five minute drive to the hospital. Julie should've been back by now.

He dug out his map of Pristina and found the southern highway. Suddenly a wave of sickness and nausea overcame him. If she'd returned that way, she would've hit the roadblock. Thoughts of her at the hands of monstrous rebel troops gripped him. He looked at her uniform hanging on the door handle and he shuddered.

Immediately he called Captain Smith and told him the story. The captain informed him that they'd had reports and that yes, there'd been hostages taken. By the time the peacekeepers had arrived, the ordeal was over. No one was around. "And I must warn you, they've been doing some pretty ugly things with the women."

Nick felt sick. Anger raged through him. He should've gone with her. A zillion thoughts flashed through his mind about where they were and what was happening to them.

"What can we do?" Nick asked.

"We'll add them to the missing person's list."

"And..."

"And there isn't much else we can do. You understand we're dealing with thousands and thousands of cases just like this. I'll get the troops to keep an eye out for the car."

His words have him a faint glimmer of hope.

Just as he hung up Julie's phone, his own rang. Nick recognized Samantha's voice.

"Nick, are you okay?"

"No, I'm not..."

"What's wrong? Do you need my help with anything?"

"My friend has been kidnapped or taken away or something by rebel troops." Nick was in a panic.

"Rebel troops? Who are they?"

"Who knows?"

"Nick, that's awful."

"No kidding. Now what am I supposed to do? She has a little kid with her too. A cute little kid."

"Where are you?"

"Still at her place."

"Oh…"

Nick recognized the tone to her voice. "She's just a friend," he yelled. "There's nothing sexual going on." He picked up the Little Noah's Ark. The words to the song by the Irish Rovers played in his mind. 'Now God seen some sinnin' and it gave him a pain. He said stand back I'm going to make it rain.' He thinks about the Quebec Flood, the Manitoba Flood, and the Mississippi flood. The earth has been changing for billions of years. Now man is in the way. What is going to happen when the earth heats up so fast from global warming and all the ice caps melt? Samantha had a couple of boats, they would be okay.

"Are you there Nick? Hello…Nick."

"Ah yeah, I'm here. Sorry, I've a lot on my mind. Some really strange things have been happening to me."

"What kind of things? Are you smoking too much weed again?"

"No, it was just one joint. It wasn't the weed. I don't have hallucinations."

"Hallucinations. What are you talking about?"

"I'm not sure. Strange things have been happening to me. Do you want to come to Kosovo?"

"What? Right. No thanks. Tell me about your hallucinations."

"I'm not having hallucinations. I'm seeing weird things."

"What kind of things?"

"Promise you won't laugh."

"I promise."

"Angels."

"Angels. You've been seeing angels? Me too."

"No way."

"Yes. Just this morning I saw one."

"Too much…"

"Aren't they committing crimes against humanity, breaching the Geneva Convention and violating the laws or customs of war over there?"

"Who?"

"The Serb leaders or whoever is killing everyone."

"Ah…yes."

"So why is it allowed to continue?"

"Ah da…Sam, are you going to come over and stop them? That's the reason for the bombs. Some people simply don't how to negotiate."

"What are they fighting about?"

"Who knows? They just kill each other. The Serbs killed some woodcutters last week so the Albanians killed two people."

"Who's winning?"

She made it sound like a poker game. "In most areas the Albanians have no rights. I met one who had an economics degree, but could never get a job. Milosevic took away all their rights and social programs all because they are of a different religion. Can you believe that?" Nick knew most Canadians don't care about what religion anyone was. They all lived together in peace and harmony, irregardless of their religion, political opinion or the color of their skin.

"It baffles me, Nick, you know, because Yugoslavia is a member of the United Nations."

"And so is Iraq. Doesn't mean a thing."

"I know, but membership in the United Nations is open to all Peace loving states. It reads like it's a prerequisite for admission. Didn't they sign that thing?"

"Probably. What are you getting at?"

"Well, the United Nations promotes and encourages respect for human rights and fundamental freedom. Some of those rights include the right to life, liberty and security of person, including freedom of religion."

"Well, it'll all be over when they charge Milosevic at The Hague for war crimes."

"I heard that it's his wife who's the powerhouse behind it all. And there's a secret police. I think they're going at it all wrong?"

"Who? What?"

"Whoever is dropping bombs. It's like treating fire with fire. They should send in the hippies."

"Get real. What are you doing these days?"

"Writing a novel."

Nick thought she was wasting her time, but didn't say so. Besides, he'd never read any of her work, so until he did, he would just keep his mouth shut. He was so schizophrenic when it came to her; one minute wanting her, the next minute wanting his freedom. They were great lovers.

Chapter Eight

Jeff leaned his gun against the side of the table, sat down, and picked up the hand of cards sitting on the table in front of him. They'd just returned from taking a large shipment of relief supplies to isolated villagers and refugees where they'd encountered a clash with Serbian forces. It hadn't been too pleasant. In the end the peacekeepers had won. The supplies had made their way to the people who needed them.

They looked up to find the captain hovering over them. "Do you remember Nick, the reporter?" The captain looked at Rick's hand. "Play that one." He pointed to the Ace of Spades.

"Yes," Jeff, Rob, and Steve answered in unison. Nick wasn't someone they'd be forgetting about too soon. His pictures were bizarre.

"He called to tell us that a friend of his has been taken by the Serbs."

"And..."

"And he was wondering if we could maybe help him try to find her. She had a small child with her."

There was a loud explosion. They ran outside into the black night to find that one of their tanks had been bombed.

"It was a rocket launcher. Look..." Steve pointed to a fleeing vehicle, "there they go."

A truck with no lights sped away down the dusty road.

"Come on, let's catch the fuckers." Five of them jumped into the Jeep and sped away. They clung tight to their rifles.

The captain watched them speed off. He looked up at the United Nations flag, the one flying outside the makeshift barracks they'd set up in an old warehouse. The flag that was supposed to be symbolic of peace. This was supposedly a safe zone.

Chapter Nine

Nick went out on to the back step and looked off into the darkness. There were no stars in the sky. It reminded him of the night he'd spent in the woods. For a moment he almost doubted his sanity and wondered if he was hallucinating. Nah, he had pictures to prove he wasn't. He wasn't sure exactly what it was he was dealing with, but whatever if was, it'd been the most beautiful thing he'd ever seen. He wanted to share it with the world, but he was afraid they'd lock him up in an asylum and throw away the key. He needed to talk to someone. He turned on his phone and was relived to hear the dial tone. He was sure the bombs were going to knock out the satellite.

"Nick, it's six in the morning. What's up?" Jack's voice sounded so familiar and wonderful.

"My friend has been kidnapped by rebels." His voice trembled.

"You're what? Who?"

"She has a friend with her."

"That's awful…Nick, you should come back. Everyone is fleeing Kosovo. It isn't safe. You must have enough information by now to write your story."

"It isn't that. It's just, well, strange things are happening to me."

"Like what?"

"Do you believe in spirits? I mean most people are non-believers until they actually have an encounter with one."

"Don't tell me you have a ghost following you."

"Not quite."

"Well, what then?"

"An angel."

"An angel. You have an angel following you?"

"Kind of. It has spoken to me and told me to do things."

"What kind of things? So have sex with it and come home."

"*Jack!* That's not funny." Nick was annoyed. "In fact, that was a sick thing to say."

"Okay. Okay, Sorry. But you have to admit it does sound weird. Invite it back home with you. Just come home. I fear for your safety."

"Tell Anita to keep playing my lottery tickets for me in the office pool."

"Yes, she's been putting money in for you every week."

"Jack..."

"Yes, Nick..."

"I have pictures."

"That's good, Nick."

"Of angels."

"What?" His voice was full of disbelief. "Well, bring them home and show them to me."

"Everyone thinks I did it with trick photography."

"And did you?"

"No."

The line was silent. "Okay, Nick. Let me get this straight. You are staying in Kosovo because there is an angel following you?"

"Something like that. Well, and now this thing with Julie."

"Have you been smoking anything?"

"Don't do this, Jack."

"What?"

"I need your support."

"You have it."

"I'll see you when I get back." He pushed the off button and threw the phone on the couch. He lay down on the bed to rest his weary bones.

A loud banging on the door frightened him. He bolted up, looked out the window, and recognized the United Nation's Jeep. He looked

110

through the peephole and recognized the two guys behind the glass. He opened the door to let Jeff and Rob in.

"I'm happy to see you guys." Nick was ecstatic. "Have you heard from Julie?"

"No. I hope they haven't taken her to the slaughterhouse."

"The what?" Nick cringed.

"Well, whatever they do with the people they kidnap. Can we come in?"

Nick opened the door for the weary boys. "Coffee?"

"We don't want to upset you Nick, but was she young and beautiful?"

"Yes."

"They maybe using her for sex."

"What? Who? What?"

"The Serb police. They just take over people's houses and stash women away for sexual purposes."

"No! She has a small child with her."

The boys looked at each other, then at Nick. "Chances are the child is dead."

Nick put his head between his hands and in his lap. "I should have gone with her. I could've prevented it."

"I don't think so. Don't blame yourself. There was probably no way you could've stopped them without being shot. If she's Albanian, she's lucky to have survived in Kosovo this long. It isn't your fault. You said she had a car?"

"A little red Toyota." He poured them both a coffee.

"We'll keep an eye out for it." They jotted down her description.

"Any chance I can come with you on patrol? I know the car and, well, don't you think it would be easier to identify if I was with you?"

Rob and Jeff studied each other. They'd had a rough day yesterday, first the stand off with the Serbs and the relief supplies. Then they'd chased a truck for about fifty miles until they'd lost it. They'd returned to the so-called barracks at two in the morning and were up again at seven. They were tired and drained. It was their fourth month in Kosovo with another two to go.

"I don't see any harm in you tagging along for the day."

Chapter Ten

Samantha watched the large fly walk across the screen in the kitchen window. It'd been buzzing around the house for days, crashing into windowpanes of glass. It was finally out of steam. She opened the screen and shooed it out. The moment it took flight, a vision came to her. She saw a young woman with long, thick, dark hair and a beautiful smile. There was a small child, approximately six years of age. Her hair in braids. Big, sad, eyes. They were in a monstrous house with many small windows. On one side of the large house was a wall with three towers, it almost looked to be a small castle. There was a little bridge beside it with a small creek that ran under. Shrubs or overgrown bush surrounded the entire building. She saw the girls in a large room, sitting on a bed. They were scared. There was hostility in the air and it was not a pleasant place to be.

Samantha didn't understand the vision. She put it aside in her mind and continued to work on her novel. It was coming along great. Nick was the main character and she couldn't wait for him to read it.

Chapter Eleven

Nick and the boys roamed the countryside in the Jeep, carefully watching for the little red Toyota.

They came upon a tractor pulling a flat bed. On it were dead bodies wrapped in white sheets. People were walking beside the flatbed in a slow death march. Women were crying.

Jeff slowed the Jeep, not wanting to pass.

"Where's Steve?"

"Italy. On leave."

"Wow. That's nice."

"One of the perks of the job, get to travel. See the world."

"Right."

The tractor pulled into a small cemetery. It was full of hastily made wooden crosses.

"Imagine all the ground water contamination from the bodies everywhere," Rob commented.

Nick shuddered. "Even body bags would help."

They slowly passed the funeral procession and headed down the road. They came to a village where people were in the dirt street hovering around burnt cars.

"What do you suppose is going on here?"

"Who knows?"

The pulled the Jeep to the side of the road. Jeff and Rob grabbed their guns and got out.

The village men climbed and sat on top of the cars. They lit their cigarettes.

"Open," Jeff demanded. He pointed to the trunk.

They sat there staring at him. Devilish grins on their faces.

"Open the damn truck," he said again and signaled to the non-English speaking people.

After some hesitation they finally agreed.

Nick watched from the Jeep.

The trunk was full of guns, small and large, and ammunition.

"Looks like we're going to have to sit here for a while," they told Nick. We have to get some backup to check this out. Chances are there are lots more where these came from." They piled the guns beside the jeep.

"I don't believe they just handed them over like that," Nick remarked.

"It isn't always that easy. We were just lucky this time. They probably figure a bomb will fall on their heads if they didn't," Rob said. The sweat poured off his brow.

Jeff radioed the sergeant who immediately dispatched a dozen men. Their role as peacekeepers meant exactly that. Keeping the peace included confiscating all guns.

As they sat in the Jeep, three young women came over and stood a small distance from them.

"I think they like us," Jeff remarked.

"Short one is cute," Rob replied.

Nick watched with envy as Jeff lit a cigarette.

"Want one?" Jeff held up the pack.

"No thanks. I don't smoke. No wonder my nerves are fried."

"No wonder."

The girls came over to the Jeep and were standing right beside them.

"You speak English?" Rob asked.

They all shrugged their shoulders. One of them went around to the other side of the Jeep and stood beside Jeff. She ran her fingers through his hair and touched him on the shoulder.

"I think she likes you," Nick told him.

She played with the collar on his shirt then walked over to a cluster of large trees, and motioned with her finger for him to come.

Rob nudged him in the rib. "She wants you big time."

Jeff looked at Rob than back at the girl. She appeared to be young and sweet. He hadn't had a woman in ages.

"Think I should?"

"Why not? Little hug and kiss won't hurt."

"What about the press in the back seat?"

"Oh, don't worry, I have my own woman back home," Nick told them.

The boys chuckled.

"Oh, what the heck. The platoon is going to be about an hour anyway. Don't fucking leave me here."

Rob started the Jeep as Jeff walked toward the girl. He turned around. "Very funny."

Rob put the Jeep into reverse, backed up a few feet then shut it off. "He knows I won't leave him."

Jeff and the girl disappeared into the bushes.

"Watch out for land mines," Rob yelled.

Nick and Rob sat still. Rob motioned for the other two girls to join them in the two vacant seats. They smiled, climbed in, and sat down. Rob knew enough Slav to ask them their names.

A fight broke out among the men who were standing outside the village pub.

"Not again!" Rob said.

"You don't have to break that up do you? Wait for back up, there's too many of them."

"I'll just go see what's going on. You stay here."

Nick watched Rob as he walked tall and proud over to the men. He fired a shot into the air.

The fighting stopped.

He returned to the Jeep. He was tall, handsome, and dignified. Nick was sure he'd a mother somewhere who was very proud. His dignified attitude was apparent.

Suddenly they heard a gun shot. Birds began to shriek and fly hysterically.

Nick's body bolted off the seat.

A high-pitched scream came from the direction of Jeff and the girl. It was the type of scream that sends chills down your spine and pierces the central nervous system. The type of scream that say's something awful has happened. They heard the sound of someone tearing through the bush.

"Holy smokes," Rob yelled. He took off into the direction. Nothing could've prepared him for what he'd found.

Jeff was still, lying on his stomach, on top of the girl. His pants were down and blood was gushing out of his back. He'd been shot in the back.

The girl was screaming and trying to push the heavy body off.

Rob scanned the area for a sniper, pulled a compress from his side pant pocket, opened it, and placed it on the wound. "Hang in there, buddy," he told him. He screamed for Nick to come.

They flipped him over. Rob checked his pulse and began cardiac resuscitation. He needed to save his friend.

"Rob, it isn't doing any good. He's gone, Rob. Time to stop."

He could hear the voice, but couldn't respond. Rob continued compressing Jeff's chest. He didn't know how long he kept it up. He collapsed beside his friend, banging the ground with his fists. "No."

Nick watched from a distance. The platoon had arrived a few minutes earlier and had shooed him out of the way.

The young girl, wrapped in a blanket, sat on the ground. Her body was trembling.

The village people had gathered around to look at the dead peacekeeper.

Nick couldn't believe the entire scenario. He'd died having sex.

"Did you take any pictures?" the sergeant asked.

"No."

"Good. Let's keep it that way. The world loves scandal. We don't need it."

Nick knew it was a hot story and the magazine would want it, but he respected their wishes. Jeff had given his life to help others. He deserved nothing but respect.

The sergeant quizzed them.

When Rob pointed to the parking lot, he realized several vehicles were now gone. "They were probably full of guns. Jeff and the girl were probably distractions for them to depart."

It was one loss for the United Nations. They would never get all the arms out of Kosovo.

"I don't know how I'm going to explain it to the family."

"Tell them he was taking a piss."

Everyone stood in somber silence as the medics loaded Jeff's lifeless body onto the stretcher. They pushed it in to the medic van and slammed the door.

Rob sat in the Jeep, choking back tears. He and Jeff had been the best of buddies. They'd met in boot camp and had been in the same platoon since joining the military some three years earlier. He picked up Jeff's little pack. Slowly and methodically he unzipped it, rummaged through the contents, and found a picture of his family. They were decent, respectable people. Someone would have the devastating task of telling them what had happened.

"Where do you want us to take you?" Rob asked Nick.

Nick wondered if this was the end of looking for Julie. "Can't I tag along with you?"

"Sure, if you still want to."

"I do. I really need to find my friend." His voice was gone again.

Chapter Twelve

Samantha watched the rain falling outside. Gently at first, then more powerful until it came down in a torrent, bashing against the window.

The vision she'd had was bothering her. Nick said his friend had a small child with her.

It had to be them. It seemed like the only plausible explanation. She had to get a message to Nick. He normally didn't believe in the mystic world, but he did say he'd seen an angel.

She dialed his number, but received the standard message that the customer was out of range.

The news was reporting that a second wave of bombs had hit Belgrade last night. Milosevic was interested in resuming diplomatic talks. NATO cancelled the bomb attacks for now. It was good news for everyone. Maybe Nick would come home soon.

Chapter Thirteen

Jack surveyed his reporters who were sitting around the table. The workweek at the *Weekly Tribute* had just started. Already he was tired. Must be a full moon.

"When is Nick returning?" Anita asked.

"Who knows? I think he's maybe on a spy mission." Jack chuckled.

"Really?" Pierre responded.

"I honestly don't know what he's up to. Claims he's seen an angel or something is following him."

A few people laughed.

"Seriously, that's what he said, also claims to have weird pictures. Anyway, I'll have to take him off the payroll soon if he doesn't hurry up. So let's get down to business? Pierre, what's going on with Microsoft?"

"They want them to split the company up."

"Why? Why take a successful enterprise and screw it up? Anyway, where's Victor?"

"Down at the old mill," Anita told him.

"Why, what's going on down there?"

"A group of developers are supposed to be in town to look at it today. They're planning to build a big resort there and tear down the old mill. Word has it the mayor has already given them the green light without public consultation."

Jack shook his head. "Okay, good place for Victor to be. Rick, you cover gas prices. Find out how high they're going to go and how the high costs will help the environment because people will use less."

Rick had a funny look on his face. "It's impossible to find that out, Jack. Should I just phone the Saudis and ask?"

"Sure. And Anita, I want you to cover the Denver story where the teen killed twelve students and a teacher."

"Why me?"

"Because you're the teacher."

"Can't you give me something a little lighter?"

"No, you're the best for this story. Find out how the kid got his hands on a gun."

She gave him an icy stare.

"And do a thing on increased violence in the youth. You know, the fact that teachers used to deal with gum chewing, hair pulling and name calling. Now they're dealing with guns, knives, gangs, and extreme violence. Just think, Anita, it's in the Rocky Mountains."

Anita smiled. "Oh, that makes me feel better." Her voice full of sarcasm.

"Michael, you get on the antibiotic dilemma. Are they overused and what should society do about it."

Jack's phone buzzed. He answered it. Spoke quickly and hung up.

"Clyde, get your team down to High Park. Another whale just beached. That's the fourth one this month. Find out why."

"When they're sick, they'll beach themselves to die."

"Okay, so find out what made them sick."

"Take my thermometer with you," Anita joked.

"Probably an oil spill." He got up and left the room.

Chapter Fourteen

Julie woke up and looked around. She was in a dark, damp basement. The bare room appeared to be an old cold storage for food. Tense with fear, she bit her hand and wished she lived in a country where stuff like this didn't happen. She didn't know how long she'd been laying there, but now she heard voices and was sure they were coming to rape her again.

Three gross, disgusting men stood at the door. "She's very beautiful."

"Take her to the east wing and clean her up."

Two young men grabbed her by the arms and yanked her to her feet.

"And leave her alone. She's for the general."

"Where's Alexis?" Julie screamed at them. "You are evil and the devil will get you."

"He is the devil." The pigs laughed. "The girl is safe."

Julie didn't believe him. "I want to see her."

"I don't take orders from you." He grabbed her arm tighter. "Take her upstairs."

He'd pulled her down a long hall and out a heavy door. Julie jumped when they shut it. She was sore and bleeding from the rapes. It was painful to walk. She heard someone say, "Wouldn't mind a round at her myself."

Julie cringed. He'd pulled her up three flights of stairs and down a nice hall with red carpet. They stopped at a beautifully carved, heavy wooden door.

"Where are we?"

"This is the new headquarters for our own little Serbian Militia. They're bombing Belgrade so we moved down here."

He led her down a beautiful hallway decorated with red carpeting and elaborate wallpaper. There was a golden statue of a boy angel. Julie wanted to reach out and touch it. He pushed a bookshelf to one side, revealing a hidden door, unlocked it, and pushed her inside. "Have a bath, bitch. The general will be here soon."

Julie entered the room. "The *general?*"

"That's right." He slammed the door.

She was amazed at the room. It was beautifully decorated with a large bed and fine furnishings. Beautiful artwork adorned the wall. A bowl of fruit sat on the side table. She began to figure it out; she was going to be the general's little fuck. "Oh God," she prayed. "Help me get out of here. Help me find Alexis."

She thought back to that fateful drive home from the hospital. She'd picked up Alexis because she was hoping to take her to Canada with her. They'd driven around a bend right into a roadblock where armed men had surrounded the car. They'd yanked them out, put them into the back of a large truck, and taped their mouths shut. They tied their hands with ropes that burned into their flesh. After driving for a bit, they were taken to the damp, cold basement and separated. Julie had been raped by three of them, over and over again. She'd been in so much pain afterwards, they'd simply left her there curled up in the corner of a dark room with nothing but a cot and pail. She wanted to die, but hung in because she had to find Alexis. She'd prayed for her safety.

She went into the large, elaborate washroom, ran a tub full of water and removed her ripped and soiled clothing. Her groin burned in searing pain. There was blood everywhere. She threw her underwear in the garbage and left her clothes in a pile on the floor. She slipped into the hot water and slumped down into the tub as far as she could go. Using the soap, she scrubbed every inch of her body, rubbing her skin briskly until it burned red. Using the soap as shampoo, she washed her hair.

As she lay there allowing the warm water to comfort her badgered soul, she heard the lock on the door turn. Tense with fear, she wondered what was going to happen next.

"Hello," a woman's voice called out.

She relaxed a degree.

"Hello," she yelled again. "I'm in the washroom."

A large, jolly, old woman appeared with a towel and robe. "The general asked me to bring you these things."

Julie was surprised. For being a prisoner, she was baffled and confused.

The woman, who looked to be someone's grandmother, had love and caring in her eyes.

Julie thanked her for the robe.

"I'll get you a hair brush and some clothing. The cook is going to bring you a hot meal. Are you related to the little girl?"

"Alexis. Have you seen her? Where is she? Is she okay?"

"She's fine. She bit one of the men and they slapped her up a bit, but other than that, she's fine. She's with the general's granddaughter."

So the men were telling her the truth. Alexis was alive and okay. Julie was relieved.

"Would you like to see her?"

"Please."

The lady smiled, walked over to the tub, and quietly whispered to her, "be nice to the general and he will treat you well. Don't cross him or he will turn on you for sure."

"What does he want with me?"

"I'm not sure, but his wife died not long ago. His daughter too. Someone shot them one night when he wasn't home." She left the room.

Julie was sitting on the edge of the bed, her hair a wet, tangled mess. She heard the key in the lock. A chill ran up her spine.

The door opened slowly.

Alexis came rushing toward her, still limping from her injuries. They embraced.

Emotions of jubilation ran through Julie.

Alexis released her grip, went to the window, and peered out to the creek below.

"What are you looking at?"

"It's far down there. Are they going to hurt us? Why are they keeping us here?"

"I don't know, honey. Hopefully we'll be okay." Julie was as scared as Alexis.

"Who was Jesus?"

The comment took her by surprise. "He was God's son."

"Why did God send a son?"

"To teach us to love. I think it was because of all the fighting and unfairness in the world."

"What happened to him?"

Did she really have to answer honestly? Alexis was young, and tender. "Pontius Pilate and a hysterical crowd of people murdered him."

"Really. Why did he do that?"

"Jesus wanted to change things. To make things fairer for everyone, and they didn't like that."

"Was Jesus the King?"

"No, he was God's son. He was sent to earth to teach people how to love one another and help the less fortunate. So, in a way, I guess he was King. He was King of people's love. He was King of love and peace."

"God must be mad about that?"

"Some people think Jesus died for our sins. I don't believe it."

"What does that mean?"

"It means that if you do something bad or stupid, God will forgive you because Jesus sacrificed himself to be a sponge for our sins? I don't buy it. Someone probably wrote that into the Holy Scriptures years ago."

"What does all that mean?"

She was at the questioning stage in life. "I say, love one another regardless of your race or religion."

"What does that mean?"

Julie smiled. "It's a long complicated story. Some people are mean and they just do mean things. It's sad, I know."

"Why do people do bad things?"

Julie brushed and braided the small child's hair. "I don't know, honey, but it isn't like that everywhere in the world. Usually only in places where mean people lead countries, when the people in power are mean."

"Why are they mean?"

Her innocence was refreshing. Children were so precious and thirsty for knowledge and guidance. "I don't know. Maybe it's all they know. Maybe it makes them feel important. Maybe their mothers were mean to them. Who know? I just wish it would change."

"Me too. Can't we just tell them to stop?"

It sounded so simple. In the eyes of a child it was simple, but for people who lacked compassion, it meant nothing.

"Has it always been like this? Have they always fought like this?

Julie wondered where the adult-like attitude in Alexis came from. "We had peace for almost thirty years, after the Second World War there was some peace."

She sat and watched the young child play with the doll she'd borrowed from the General's daughter. Julie was captivated by the innocence of youth.

"I'm going to get dressed," Julie told her.

While putting on her bra, she heard voices coming from the other room. She returned to Alexis, looked around but saw no one.

"Who were you talking to?"

"My guardian angel."

"Your guardian angel?"

"Yes, she follows me everywhere I go."

Julie smiled. Probably just an imaginary childhood friend. She thought about Nick and his experience with angels. She didn't believe it.

Chapter Fifteen

At the base on American soil, the lieutenant was sitting behind his desk flipping through the budget. More cuts to personnel and an increase to the artillery budget. The high price of firepower. The attacks on Kosovo over the last fifteen days of the air strikes had cost the United States close to five-hundred million dollars. The Canadian figures weren't in yet.

His phone rang. "Lieutenant Stephenson," he answered.

"Bill, it's Gary over here in Kosovo."

The lieutenant could tell by the sound of his voice that it wasn't good news.

"We have causality. Sniper fire in the woods."

The lieutenant hated receiving such news. "What happened?"

"Unknown sniper got him while he was taking a piss."

"No shit? What a way to go. Where?"

"Little Village outside Pristina. We figure it to be a distraction so some vehicles carrying arsenal could get away."

"Did you hear the news?"

"About what?"

"The bombing have been postponed for now. We think Milosevic has finally buckled."

It was sweet music to Gary's ears, but would it mean peace? Milosevic's human rights violations of massacring innocent people may finally come to an end.

The base commander watched the American flags flying half-mast from his office window. They flopped in the wind. Even though the war was halfway around the world, he felt as though he was standing right in it.

A group of young recruits were at its base practicing a morning drill, saluting their sergeant.

He was waiting the arrival of the family liaison officers. The ones who delivered the death notices.

He watched the flag flap, fall and flap again.

The door opened. "Good morning, sir," he heard them say. They took their seats and helped themselves to his three candy jars full of treats that sat on the corner of his vast desk.

Without a word he handed them the list.

They climbed the steps to the elegant family home of Jeff Peterson and knocked on the door.

A small child of about four years of age, with long blonde hair and blue eyes answered. She stretched her neck to look up at the tall men in uniform.

"Is your mommy or daddy home?"

Quickly the child slammed the door in their faces and shouted, "Mom, there's men at the door. Some men at the door."

The waited patiently for ten minutes then rang the doorbell. Chimes echoed. A few minutes later the door opened. An attractive woman stood before him. Before they had a chance to speak, she put her hand to her mouth and screamed, "No."

They nodded their heads. Nigel put his hand on her shoulder. "Afraid so."

Two young girls were tugging on their mother's clothing. "Come on, Mom." They tugged her inside. "Did something happen to Jeff?" one of them asked.

"Yes, honey." She looked at the officers. "How? How did it happen?" Her voice trembled.

"He was going to the washroom in the woods. An unidentified sniper shot him from behind. It was a distraction thing. We believe they did it to escape with arms."

"Going…going to the washroom? He was shot while having a pee?"

"That's the report we have, madam."

"Of course. Oh, my God," she screamed. She stood up and paced around. "Oh no, he's never coming back. We're never going to see him again."

The small children curled up together on the couch.

"Can we call someone for you?"

She sat down. "No. I'll be okay. Thank you."

"Are you sure?"

"Yes."

"We'll forward documents regarding the arrival of his body."

Her eyes widened. "Thank you."

"Are you sure you don't want us to stay a while?"

"No, I'll be fine." She walked them to the door and shut it. They heard a long, deep scream.

Mrs. Peterson was shattered. Jeff was their only son. Because some asshole on the other side of the world had shot her first born a family would be changed forever.

Mr. and Mrs. Mrs. Peterson stood beside the coffin as the priest committed Jeff's body to the earth. Ashes to ashes and dust to dust. On each side of them stood Jeff's two younger sisters, tears rolling down their angelica faces.

Mrs. Peterson, weak at the knees, held her composure.

Two soldiers removed the flag from the coffin, folded it, and presented it to Jeff's mother.

The priest continued, "Jeff died in the struggle for peace on our sickened planet. He died in the fight for human rights."

Mrs. Peterson thought about how totally senseless it all was. They could've shot him in the leg or something. They didn't have to kill him. She knew all the agonizing and hypothesizing would never bring her son back. The child that'd grown inside her womb, the child she'd nurtured, loved and raised. The son she'd loved with all her heart and soul would never come home. Instead, his body would decompose into nothing but bones. It would be a loss she would never recover from.

Chapter Sixteen

Nick opened his eyes to find a face peering down on him.

"I nearly croaked. I thought you were Jeff," the young solider told him.

"I guess that's what I get for sleeping in a dead person's cot."

The solider laughed. "Who are you?"

Nick told him about Julie and his desires to find her and the child.

"You're Nick."

"Yes."

"That's awful about Jeff. He never had a chance." He turned and sauntered across the room.

Nick watched him. He wondered how many more innocent lives would be lost before it was all over.

The sergeant walked into the barracks and looked around. "Okay, everyone, time to rise and shine. We have new orders from the captain. From now on, everyone is to wear their protective vests. No more repeats of what happened yesterday. Do not remove it for any reason."

The barracks was silent.

Chapter Seventeen

Anita threw the massacre story on Jack's desk. "Here it is!" she yelled.

"Don't sound so enthused. How was Denver?"

"Denver was fine, but I can't deal with this type of reporting any more. I want to do a story on peace."

Jack looked at her carefully, analyzing the lines on her face. The way her smile, the one where the corners of her lips were usually turned upward, now turned down. Her brow was furrowed above her eyes. Jaw clamped tight. "What happened?" Jack wondered what put her in such a mood. He flipped through the story. "This is good."

"Nothing happened!" she screamed at him. "I'm sick of writing about stuff like this. I want to write about peace."

"Peace? Peace won't sell." Jack had seen it before. Reporters come back from emotionally draining assignments, spin out for awhile, calm down, and return for more. It was all part of the job.

"What do you mean peace won't sell?"

Jack stared straight into her eyes. "Just what I said. I've been the editor here for twenty years. I know what will sell and what won't. I'm telling you, peace won't sell. It's nothing."

"*Nothing!* Do you think everyone on this planet wants to read about grief and agony? Maybe people are getting sick of it. Maybe everyone would like a change. Have you ever thought about that?"

"Anita, take some time off then come back and see me." He buried his head in his work.

131

She bellowed, "No more violence! Find me something sickly sweet to do, let me do a story on peace or I'm out of here." She spun and headed out the door.

Jack picked up a page and waved it in the air. "This is really good!" he shouted. He figured she'd calm down in a day or two. "Go home, have a few drinks, you'll be good as new on Monday." Jack picked up his phone and pushed the yellow button. "Hold the press," he told Sue. "I have something for the front page." He really did like the story. She'd reached into the lives of the families of the victims. It was written in a manner that moved the reader. She was good. Anita had learnt from investigators that the boys owned an astonishing arsenal of weapons that included firearms and homemade bombs.

There had been many warning signs that the two boys were deeply disturbed. There were no problems until grade eleven when they started wearing black, keeping to themselves and hanging out with a gang of twenty students who called themselves the Trench-coat Mafia. They hated the preppies, jocks and clean cut kids. They listened to music with destructive suicidal themes and death cult music. They identified with the Gothic culture of black clothing and makeup. The jocks put them down.

A youth-offender court official described them as being bright and with potential. It was all a misconception. Even while excelling in an anger management course they were out of control. The two were fascinated with violent computer games and had made a video where they talked about blowing up the school and all of Denver. The video was shown in class where no one saw it as a threat.

Some kids took them serious, others didn't. One sixteen-year-old female feared them. "They would go around saying they were going to take over the world." Some kids were angry, saying they were out of control and no one did anything about it. They marched around the school elbowing people and threatening to kill people. One student had even told police that they were making pipe bombs and had a threatening web site. No one did anything about it.

The neighbors reported seeing them holed up in the garage for hours. Everyone wanted to know where their working professional parents were when all this was happening? Their kids had tons of guns, were making bombs and the parents didn't notice?

The county district attorney talked about how he felt our mass media desensitizes kids to violence; real live sex and blood soaked movies. There was a general pollution of violence in our mass media.

The scariest thought of it all was that it was occurring in North America. One of the greatest nations on earth was producing violent teens without feeling or remorse. Maybe the loss of the traditional buffers of extended families, religion, and community was a reason. The kids were relying on one another.

One thing was clear was that if kids are obsessed with violence or killing, parents shouldn't dismiss it as merely a phase.

She felt there definitely was a need for stricter gun control and that authorities needed to take threats move seriously and quit waiting before it's too late to do something. Sometimes just a visit from the Police is enough to deter delinquent behavior.

He put the paper down. Time to check the lottery numbers. If his eyes weren't deceiving them, they'd just won the jackpot. He quickly called the smoke shop where they'd purchased the ticket and had them verify the numbers.

"How much?"

"Wasn't too high last night. Maybe one and a half."

"One and a half *million?*"

"Something like that."

Jack grabbed his calculator. He divided it by four. It was about three-hundred and seventy five-thousand each. Good thing Anita was paying for Nick's tickets while he was away. Better not tell him, he might never return.

Anita opened the door to her tastefully decorated apartment, crashed onto the couch and stared blankly at the pictures hanging on the wall.

Jack's words kept going through her mind: *Peace won't sell. Peace won't sell.*

She was determined to prove him wrong. What was peace? According to Webster's dictionary and from among several definitions, she found that peace was "a state of tranquility" and "freedom from civil disturbance." Peace was "a state or period of mutual concord between governments." Peace was "harmony in personal relations."

She turned on the television. There was another IRA bombing in Ireland. She turned off the TV, picked up the paper and flipped though it. Something in the far corner of the page caught her eye. It was small, but her subconscious memory took it into its processing center. A spark ignited her brain. It was a little candle with a flame swirling around it. A little bright flicker of light. Below were the words, Amnesty International. The caption read: *Help the Prisoners of Torture.*

Later, on her shopping spree, she thought about all the places around the globe where people were being shot, slaughtered, tortured, hungry, and in terrific emotional and physical pain, living in non-sustainable environments with little population control and insane governments.

Human rights of the most distraught kind were being violated every second of every day somewhere in the world.

Chapter Eighteen

"We're never going to find her, you know that, right?" the driver told Nick after driving all day and looking for the red Toyota.

"I can't give up. I know she's alive. I can feel it in my bones. Besides, I feel lucky today."

Rob spit out his coffee. "*Lucky,*" he smirked. "How could anyone be *lucky* around here?"

It'd been an emotionally draining day. They'd discovered another mass grave and had to chase away wild dogs. They'd helped load bodies into a truck. The bodies were taken to a field where articles of clothing or jewelry were attached to the bags to help families recognize their loved ones. Unidentified articles and pieces of clothing would be compiled in a large manual coordinated by the International Community of the Red Cross's Humanitarian Services division and kept forever until someone identified it. The bodies were then tagged and their names added to the long list of death notices.

The country was a mess. The bombs had made an impact everywhere. Destruction was more the norm than the rule. It would take years to rebuild what they once had.

"Why are all the rooftops red?" Nick asked as they passed several houses on the mountainside.

"Haven't quite figured that one out yet," Bruce said, looking up at the houses, some of which were burnt to the ground.

"I need a drink," Nick said. "Let's find a bar."

"Good plan." Rob drove to the down town section. The dust and rubble in the streets made their eyes water. He stopped in front of a shabby old building. "Stripper?"

"Fine by me," Bruce said.

Nick was quiet. It wasn't quite what he had in mind but it would do. "Sure anything. He pulled his press tag out of his pocket, looked at if for a second, and then shoved it back.

Pretending to be hiding behind a dumpster, the boys changed out of their uniforms and into street clothes.

Arriving at the door they were instantly surrounded by a small gang of youths. One of them held a finger in a gun pointing manner and shot at them.

Nick turned. "Hey."

The youths quickly scattered away laughing.

The place was crowded for five thirty in the afternoon. The stench of cigarette smoke and spilled drink was in the air. They ordered their beverages.

The stripper was very attractive, wearing a sequence of glittery stones on her bikini top and bottom. She sparkled in the lights and moved gracefully to the music. Her face was sad. She faked a smile.

Nick was enchanted by the way she moved. She had to be a trained dancer.

Bruce and Rob were slugging back the brew. "Can you drive, Nick?" Rob asked.

Rob and Bruce were officially off duty at five. They were sure the captain would understand when they didn't return the Jeep. It would be one of those things. They would just do it and get in shit for it later.

"She's good," Nick commented, watching the dancer moved to the rhythm. "Not only can she dance, but she's beautiful."

"Oh yeah. She's cute."

The thirsty boys slugged back the drinks.

Nick was mesmerized with the dancer. She was a vision of elegance in the middle of so much despair. She moved with grace.

A large troop of noisy British peacekeepers entered. They found their seats.

Nick thought about all the corrupt politicians they'd assisted in overthrowing over the decades. The Brits were always willing to help.

Nick grew a bulge and wished Samantha was around. He would love to have sex with her right now.

The dancer finished her act and someone else came on stage.

Nick had to meet her. He wanted to interview her.

"I'll be right back."

Rob and Bruce noticed the bulge in his pant. They laughed.

Nick staggered toward the washroom, went into a stall and whipped it out. Quickly and with precision, he jerked off into the toilet. The tension left his body. Relieved, he zipped up and clipped his press I.D. onto his shirt.

He went to the bar and found an English speaking bartender.

"I would like to interview the stripper for the paper I work for. She's no ordinary dancer. I just want to talk to her for a minute. Can you arrange it?"

"What paper? Where from?"

"The *Tribute*. Vancouver, Canada. "

The bartender pulled the ID off his shirt pocket, read it, then threw it on the counter. "Wait here."

After a long wait, he returned. "She'll meet with you in the hallway." He gave Nick directions.

He walked down the long hall and found her standing outside the dressing room.

"Where did you go?" Rob asked Nick as he returned to the table.

"I interviewed that stripper."

"You did what?" They both chuckled.

"I interviewed the stripper. She's going to join us after her last act."

Rob and Bruce smiled. "So…so tell us already, how'd it go?"

"She's a professional ballerina and modern dancer who ended up stripping because of the economy," Nick said. His voice going on him again.

137

They sat for a few minutes watching the dancer.

Suddenly Rob blurted out, "I'm going to find that son-of-a-bitch who put a bullet in Jeff's back. When I do, watch out."

Bruce and Nick were taken back by the sudden mood swing in Rob.

"It isn't fair. It just isn't fair!" he shouted.

"These things happen," Nick tried to comfort him. "It's painful, I know, but these things happen."

"I'm going to find the fucker, you watch."

Bruce shoved his drink toward him. "Have a drink of rum."

After a few gulps, he calmed down.

They watched the next two shows and then, as promised, the stripper came to their table. She'd changed into her street clothes.

Nick introduced her to his friends. "This is Marcia."

"You look different with clothes on," Rob commented.

She gave him a funny look.

"Don't mind him. He's in shock," Bruce said.

The waiter brought her a large drink. She gulped half of it.

"I may be Serb," she said, "but I certainly do not approve of what has been happening. This is an awful way to live. This is no life." She spoke with emotion.

The boys really felt for her. She was a beautiful and talented woman who wanted nothing but to be a professional dancer on the international stage, to dance for audiences who wore long gowns and tuxedos, who appreciated art form and culture. She wanted to dance for the intellectual, the rich and famous. The money was good. It was the only work she could get during a war she didn't want. A war few wanted. A war forced on so many. Something was definitely wrong.

"It may all be over soon," Rob said. "There haven't been any bombings for days, peace is on the way."

"We'll never have peace as long as Milosevic is in power."

"Why do the people vote him in?" Bruce asked.

"He came into power in 1987 as head of the Serbian Communist party. It was when the Soviet empire had crumbled. Then he became the Serb President in 1989 and served two terms. He was barred from a third term so he rewrote the constitution in 1997 to transfer real power to the Yugoslav presidency of Serbia and Montenegro. Then the country's M.P.'s voted him into that job in an indirect election. He's now in power until the end of the year 2000. He promised a greater Serbia, but has only given us war and ruin.

Since 1987, Croatia, Bosnia, Macedonia, and Slovenia have broken away from the Yugoslav Federation. Thousands of Serbs have died fighting losing battles. How long must the ten-million people of Serbia be under rule of a war criminal?"

"He's now considered an outcast on the global front. Any new government will probably hand him over to the war crimes prosecutors," Nick told them.

"There's a rumor that he's been bringing money to Yugoslavia from Panama, Greece, and China to keep the regime going. He wants to keep a bad economy so the people are too poor to survive and therefore won't turn against him. Keeping the sanctions is his key to staying in power," her voice full off discouragement.

"Sanctions. What's that? I know the word, I just forget what it means." Bruce was young.

Rob was used to his naiveté.

"It's when someone has violated international law. An economic or military measure is taken. Most times it means they can't get supplies from outside the country," Rob told him.

"And now we are a poor country. We are weaker and smaller than ever before," the dancer told them. Her eyes were full of sorrow. "It's sad. Really sad, and it certainly isn't something the people want. The war has taken ten years off of my life. We live in constant waiting and anticipation for it to end." Her voice quivered. "Sometimes I really question NATOs' decision to bomb. I mean, it seems that they are aiming at the very people they are here to protect. I mean, what role does the United Nations play in all of this?"

Nick looked at her. She didn't know. The United Nations didn't authorize it. NATO hadn't asked for permission to attack because they knew they wouldn't get it."

Nick tried to explain it rationally. "Mr. Blair, the British Prime Minister said, 'We cannot turn our backs on the violation of human rights in other countries.' The bottom line is that innocent people were dying and forced to leave their homes. There didn't appear to be any end to it. Your leader is a madman, plain and simple. As far as the United Nations go, they failed to prevent the mass genocide in Rwanda. In fact, they found eleven slaughtered peacekeepers. Where was the United Nations in Bosnia? They failed there too. Basically, NATO intervened when no one else would or could. Basically, it's all bullshit if you ask me. Who cares what the reasons are, bottom line is that it's just people killing people. They are violating two of the Ten Commandments 'Thou shalt not kill' and 'Thou shall love thy neighbor.'"

Everyone was silent. Nick was right. As long as there were madmen in control in countries where human rights were being violated, someone would have to intervene on their behalf. The good cannot turn its back on evil and allow it to continue. Who wants to sit back and just watch innocent people be tortured and killed and not do anything?

"The Balkan Wars have been going on forever. There were two wars back in the early 1900s that damaged European alliances and helped spark the outbreak of the first World War," Marcia told them.

"And what happened in Bosnia not too long ago?" Bruce asked.

"In the early 1990s the Serbs tried to mold a mini-state out of Bosnia. More than 200,000 people were killed and 20,000 women raped. It was awful. They took truckloads of men and boys out to an old abandoned school house and shot them with submachine guns. It happened in Srebrenica, a place that was declared a UN safe haven.

Bosnian Serb forces just took over after a day of artillery fighting. About a thousand people surrendered to the Serb troops who promised to treat them within the rules of the Geneva Convention. That promise was broken."

"The Geneva Convention. What's that?" Bruce asked. "I forget."

"I did an article on the Red Cross at one time," Nick told them. "It was the members of the Red Cross who signed the first Geneva

Convention. In 1864, a Swiss philanthropist named Jean Henri Dunant was appalled by the almost complete lack of care for wounded soldiers, so he founded the Red Cross. Several members of the Swiss Red Cross signed the ground rules for the treatment of the wounded and for protection of medical personnel and hospitals. That was the first Geneva Convention."

"I know that guy," Rob said. "He won the first Nobel Peace Prize way back in the early 1900s."

"You got it," Nick said. "I did an article on the Nobel Peace Prizes too. They are purchased from the accrued interest on a trust fund of the Swedish chemist, inventor and philanthropist, Alfred Bernhard Nobel. The winners get a cash reward, a gold medal and diploma. There are five fields of recognition: physics, chemistry, physiology, medicine, literature, international peace and economic science. In 1988 the United Nations peacekeeping forces were awarded the Nobel Peace Prize."

"And who or what is NATO?" Marica asked.

"It is called the North Atlantic Treaty Organization and it was formed in 1949 by a bunch of countries that saw Russia as a threat to peace after World War II. Russia was doing things that looked like they were headed toward World War III. Basically, it's a collective military unit from all around the world. Their first article of the Treaty calls for a peaceful resolution to disputes. That never happened over here, which is why they resorted to the bombing."

"There are fourteen articles to that thing. Some people really question whether or not they followed their own rules," Rob told them.

"What do you mean?" Marcia asked.

"You're the walking dictionary, Nick, you tell her," Rob said.

"Article four calls for a joint consultation when a member is threatened. This war was an internal thing. You guys were killing each other. NATO came to protect the innocent because no one else could. The United Nations would never approve of something like that because they were established to maintain international peace and security. Their members pledge to fulfill obligations of international cooperation and settle disputes by peaceful means and refrain from the threat or use of force. The United Nations is having a hard time keeping up with the madmen of the world. When United Nations peacekeepers are turning up dead, well then, something is really wrong."

Everyone sat back.

Nick took a deep breath. His voice was almost gone again. There was so much involved, but basically, if everyone could just learn to love one another instead of killing each other then we wouldn't need organization like NATO. Nick was really glad that NATO existed because he was sure that without them, the entire planet might be at war.

"It's too bad that it is this way here. It's such beautiful country. Tourism could probably be a big industry. Who wants to visit a war zone on their holidays? This is suicide what's going on," Bruce said.

Nick thought about his angel and the message he'd received in the field that night. "This is your sign, Nick. Take this with you in your quest for peace, freedom and human rights." He still wasn't sure what he was supposed to do with that message, but he would figure something out someday. He had to.

Chapter Nineteen

Julie peered out the window to the river below. She was a prisoner in a castle and didn't understand. Many days had gone by and still the general had not paid her a visit. She considered herself lucky to be locked in such a beautiful place when so many people were being violently victimized and brutalized by the war. She thought about all the awful things that were going on around the world. In China, they execute you for the most minor of crimes. In India, children are slaves to the work force. Turkey is one of the most violent places on earth. In Sudan, African people were being slaughtered every second of the day. In Iraq, a madman tortured prisoners of war and executed his own people. That was just the tip of the iceberg. In Mexico, people were being pulled over and shot for no reason. Is this human rights? Why was it happening? Why couldn't it be stopped? She wished so much someone could put an end to it all. She wondered if Nick had returned to Canada.

The housekeeper came into the room. "The general would like to see you." She set a dinner tray on the side table.

A crushing feeling hit the pit of her stomach. "Where's Alexis!" she yelled.

"They're playing in the courtyard."

She felt herself relax for a few seconds.

"The general will be here shortly," she said gently and left the room.

Julie's muscles tightened. This was the dreaded moment. The seconds slowly passed. The anticipation was causing an anxiety of mental anguish and fear so intense she began to gag. She thought about Roeg, her boyfriend who was killed so violently because of his quest for human rights. The emptiness inside her since his death was still there. It would probably never leave.

She heard the door creak open.

The general stood in the doorway.

She thought he was the devil. He had the look of Satan. She was convinced the devil had possessed the souls of every evil terrorist on the planet.

The housekeeper's words kept echoing in the back of her mind. She decided to cooperate with this asshole so maybe she could get out alive.

"I don't want to hurt you," he told her. "I'm only in need of personal satisfaction. Stress release, you know what I'm saying?"

Julie sat in silence.

"Please remove your clothing."

She stood from the chair she'd been sitting in, undid her blouse, slowly removed it, revealing her youthful, firm, rounded breasts.

The general became instantly aroused.

She removed her skirt and carefully laid it over the back of the chair. Slowly, without thought, she took off her underwear.

The General removed his clothing.

She cringed at the sight of his large swollen penis. It was going to be painful. She wasn't the least bit aroused.

He motioned with his eyes to the bed and Julie obeyed. She pulled back the sheet and lay on the bed. Her legs bent.

He crawled on, pulled her legs apart, and entered her.

As expected, the pain was intense. He ripped into her dry vagina and rammed fiercely. She wanted to die. He had his stinky, repulsive tongue over her mouth. He told her she was nice and tight and it felt good for him. His words made her sick.

She lay motionless as he rammed into her over and over again. His powerful thrusting pounded her groin. She wanted to scream, but would spare him the thrill of having a screamer. Some men liked screamers. It motivated them to orgasm. Maybe she should just scream and get it over with.

She grabbed the bed sheet and looked at the picture on the wall. It was a painting of a boat off in the distance. A rocky shoreline. She wanted to be on that boat, sailing far out to sea.

Finally she screamed. It worked. He came. A loud grunt and he collapsed on top of her. He lay there for a minute when Julie finally said, "Please, I can't breathe."

He rolled off.

The scent of his perspiration was everywhere. He smelt of cigars and liquor.

Julie closed her eyes and wondered where Nick was. She wished he would find her and take her home to his wonderful country with him.

After he left, she curled up in the hot water of the bath and cried. Large tears splashed into the water. She watched the ripples make their way to the side of the tub.

She asked God to help Nick find her.

Chapter Twenty

Nick stopped the Jeep in front of Julie's house and thanked Bruce and Rob for the interesting evening. They'd spent the night in some fleabag hotel room. Now he was feeling queasy. He hadn't drunk all that much, but was feeling the effects of the cigarette smoke and not enough sleep.

"Why don't you come in for a while?" Nick asked. "It's your day off, isn't it?"

Rob and Bruce both smiled. "Sure, why not? We're already in big trouble for not returning the Jeep. They will be looking for it for patrol. Beats going back to our depressing living room."

Nick found the key exactly where he'd left it. He slowly opened the door. In a place like Kosovo, it couldn't hurt to be too cautious. They took a quick look in all the rooms. He decided everything was fine, nothing had been touched. Nick checked his gear, relieved to find everything was as he'd left it. Most importantly his pictures of the angels were still there.

"Nice place," Rob said. He slumped down in a chair.

Nick put on a pot of coffee. His phone made a clicking noise. He picked it up but it wasn't working. "Wonder what that's all about?"

"Could be a damaged satellite. Sometimes they work enough to get a signal but aren't strong enough to pick up a message."

If someone was trying to phone him, it could only be two people, either Samantha or Jack. He laughed at the thought of Samantha calling him. She never gave up on him. Even when he'd been a real prick she'd run back for more.

Nick handed the boys a hot cup of coffee. He cooked eggs and toast.

"What will you do now?"

"I'll probably go back home soon, even though I feel uneasy about leaving like this, not knowing where Julie is."

"We'll continue to keep an eye out for her," Rob promised.

"Thanks," Nick said sincerely. There was an uneasy calm. Everyone knew what the other was thinking. Julie could very well be dead right now because she was an Albanian who'd been picked up by the Serbs.

"I should inform her family I guess," Nick said. "She must have the number here someplace."

Nick found their name in the automatic dial on the phone. The answering machine came on. He left a message for them to contact the captain.

Nick bade goodbye to Rob and Bruce and watched them drive away. The house now felt like a mortuary. He decided to try and phone Samantha. It rang several times before she answered, huffing and puffing from doing aerobics.

"Nick!" she screamed. "Where are you?"

"Still in Kosovo." He wished he wasn't.

"I've been trying to get a hold of you. I had a vision."

Nick wondered about her sometimes. "Now what?"

"I'm sure it's your girlfriend."

"She isn't my girlfriend."

"Well, whoever or whatever she is. She's in a big monstrous house with many small windows. On one side of the house there's a wall with three towers. Looks like a castle. Little bridge beside it with a small creek running under it. There are lots of shrubs around and the bush is overgrown. I saw a girl with long dark hair and a little girl with her hair in braids."

Nick was silent. She was describing Julie and Alexis. He knew she had some psychic powers because she'd said some pretty strange things before that had come true. "Really? Anything else?"

"No, that's it. How are you doing?"

"I'm okay."

"I just want you to know that I've given up on any idea that you may be back. I've accepted the fact we are never going to have a relationship."

Nick was stunned. He'd been thinking about her lately and was beginning to really need her. He needed the emotional strength she gave him. He wasn't capable of a relationship, but he needed comforting.

Chapter Twenty-One

Anita pulled on her skirt then peered at herself in the mirror. Her executive style suit made her look elegant, refined, and professional. She was starting back to work today. It was going to be interesting. She'd made up her mind that she was no longer taking orders from Jack, her boss, who gave all the orders. From now on she was going to work on whatever stories she felt like. At the same time, she didn't want to lose her job because she'd grown to love some of the people. She wished Nick would get back. She was really missing his smile. He had a beautiful smile. It pulled into the side of his jawbones, wrapped around his face.

It was going to be an interesting day because Jack was not going to like what she had to say.

She revved up her old truck, the eighteen-year-old Chevy that just kept on running. It was costing her money but she loved the old truck. It still got her places.

It was a quick drive. She pulled into the parking lot. The parking attendant, who never spoke, handed her a day pass. Just get your ticket and get going. Anita figured he hated his job. It would be nice to talk about the weather with him someday, but he was never interested.

She walked into Jack's office.

He was sitting behind his desk reading something. Quietly she sat down, waiting for him to acknowledge her. Without lifting his head, he stuck his index finger into the air. Finally, after what seemed to be an eternity, he looked up.

"Good morning."

"Yes. It's a nice morning."

"The meeting is at ten." He didn't look well.

"I want to talk to you about something."

"Well, make it quick because we're about to lose the Rivlon ads." He put his hand on the receiver.

Anita knew what that meant. They'd been carrying the Rivlon ads for almost twenty years. The account was worth millions. "People wear too much makeup anyway."

Jack gave her an evil glare.

"Okay, so here goes, real quick. Have you ever heard of the good manager who knows when to step aside and let their employees do their jobs?"

"Is this going somewhere?"

"Free reign. I want to do whatever I want. Starting now." She watched the expression on his face. It went from weird to weirder.

"Fine," he finally said. His buzzer rang. He picked it up. He listened for a few seconds, hung it up, and stood up. "I have to go to Leroy's office for a minute. Watch the phone for me, will you? Shelley is puking again." He went out the door, not giving her a chance to say no.

Poor Shelley. She'd been pregnant for two months and had thrown up every single day.

Anita sat in Jack's comfortable chair. She twirled around a few times, checking the view of the skyscraper next door, remembering when they had a commanding view of the ocean, now it was a skyscraper. Everyone had been in a real bad mood afterwards.

She picked up the layout for this week's cover. Microsoft was appealing the judge's decision to break the company up. She hadn't really been following the story closely, but as far as she could see, the judge was trying to prevent a huge conglomerate from having a monopoly.

The phone rang. "Jack Jam's office."

The line was momentarily silent. Then she heard the familiar voice, "Anita?" It was Nick.

"Nick, I'm so happy to hear your voice. How are you?"

"Good. Well, sort of good. I feel okay, but this place is hell."

"I take it you are still in Kosovo. What's taking so long?"

"Stuff keeps happening."

"How's your angel?" She wanted to laugh but refrained. She knew what assignments like that could do to a person.

"Haven't seen her around lately."

"You're probably looking for Jack. He'll be back in a minute. Give me your number…"

"No, it's okay. I just need to talk to someone."

"Well, I'm someone. When are you coming back? Did you hear we won the lottery?"

"What!"

"Seriously. About four-hundred thousand each."

"No way. Wow!"

"And guess what?"

"What?"

"Jack gave me free rein to do whatever story I want. I'm going to write about peace."

"He did? Wow, that's sure not like him. You're going to write about peace?"

"Yup. Starting today."

"So am I. Good luck."

"What? I thought you were covering the war."

"I am. It's bullshit. I've had a spiritual encounter."

"I heard about that. The angel. So is she for peace too?" Anita didn't quite know what to say. She'd never had a spiritual encounter and was a bit of a skeptic.

"I have some ideas. We should work together. I'm coming back soon. I just have to take care of one more thing. A friend has been kidnapped by the rebels."

"Oh no! Are you serious?"

"Yes."

"That's awful. So what are you going to do about this peace thing?"

"I haven't decided yet. Hopefully the spirits will guide my way."

Anita chuckled. Maybe he was losing it, who knew for sure? "There certainly are a lot of peace organizations around. The United Nations, Red Cross, Amnesty International…" Her mind took a nosedive into the depths of her brain, the wheels of thought churning a hundred miles an hour.

Chapter Twenty-Two

"Where have you been with that Jeep?" The captain was yelling at them. He looked pissed. "The boys are waiting for someone to pick them up at the dock in Albania. They had to take the supply truck."

They'd forgotten some were returning from leave in Italy today. "Sorry, we got sidetracked."

"And Nick just called…"

"Nick, we just left him."

"Apparently some friend of his has had a vision about where Julie and the kid are."

A vision. Bruce and Rob laughed. "What next?"

"He wants us to keep an eye out for a castle," he said, and described what Nick had told him.

"There's a place similar to that down by the textile plant along the river," Bruce said. "I remember seeing it and thinking it was spooky."

"There is?" the Captain responded. "That's interesting."

"I think it's located right about there." Bruce pointed to a spot on the map.

The captain jumped in to the driver's seat. "Let's go."

Bruce had almost been right. They'd no trouble finding the place. It was visible from across the river. They drove by, pretending not to notice anything. A large truck pulled up, disappeared behind the bushes, then totally out of sight. It was no ordinary house. It was a small castle.

They returned to base, changed into civilian clothes and picked up the unmarked car. Time for some detective work.

They climbed the mud soaked mountain path to the large one-hundred sixty-five-year-old Muslim, Albania farm. Kosovo is seventy-percent mountains. Almost everywhere you go there is a hill to climb up or down. They looked at the old watermill. This village was virtually self-sufficient. They had cattle, poultry, good crops of wheat, corn, peppers, and cabbage. They climbed the large stone staircase to the house.

"Bahhh," Rob bawled at a white goat that was nibbling on thorn bushes out in the field.

The kind old lady who lived there invited them in. A warm fire burned in an iron stove, water dripped from the cracks in the limestone walls making the floor a big puddle.

"Hey, Bessie, Can we take your dog for a walk?" the captain asked. They knew her well because she sold wildflowers from an old metal drum at the end of the road. She was always baking sweet things to eat and would walk around the small hills in front of her house handing out baked good to the boys. She tolerated the situation well, the sophisticated, supertech, airplanes that dropped tons of ordnance night after night.

Bessie looked down at the fifteen-year-old dog. "You want to walk that old thing?"

"Day off. Just feel like walking a dog down by the river, you know, something exciting to do."

She laughed. "Oh, that's real excitement. You go right ahead."

"Get in the car, Champ."

The old pooch obeyed the lady when she opened the door. He watched her from the back seat as they drove away, tongue hanging out, and a big smile on his face. Yahoo, going for a ride.

Ryan stroked his head. "Nice doggy. Yes, you are a nice doggy." Everyone on the base knew the old dog. He wandered the hills looking for anyone who would give him a pat and a friendly word and would cover his face with his paws anytime there was a blast.

They followed the rugged path along the river until they had a view of the driveway. Champ retrieved the ball a few times then lay down and wouldn't move.

They saw a man with a rifle walk to the front of the truck and sit on the fender. He lit a cigarette.

"I've seen enough. Let's go," the captain said.

"What's the plan?" Rob asked the captain.

"We need to get someone undercover on the inside. I'm going to ask Milikia to help us on this one."

Everyone knew Milikia. He was a Serb who hated what was going on. He wanted to help the peacekeepers any way he could.

"He's out at the wood lot. I saw him leaving this morning," Barry said.

"Go fetch him."

Berry and Steve quickly jumped into the Jeep and headed out.

"What was it like in Nam?"

Everyone knew Steve had done time in Vietnam, but he rarely talked about it.

"It's a beautiful, rugged mountainous country with coastal plains and river deltas. The rice patties and cotton fields are breathtaking."

"Why did the Americans go? Everyone says they stuck their noses in where it didn't belong."

"That's not true. The war began because the North wanted to overthrow the South. Forty other countries supported the South by supplying them with troops and munitions. Russia and China were helping the North. It was the civilians who felt the brunt of it." He remembered the kids in the jungle, young boys with rifles, fear on their faces. It wasn't something he cared to remember or think about.

The road to the wood lot was windy and bumpy. They rode in silence for most of the drive. It didn't take them long to find Milikia. He was throwing wood onto the back of his truck and turned around when he heard them coming. He dropped a big log in its place and smiled at the boys. His expression was a mixture of happiness and wonder.

"The captain needs your help on something."

"Do you know what for?"

"No, but they're going on a hunch about a castle down by the textile plant."

"That place has been empty for years."

"Well, not anymore, we think they're running guns through it."

The anger brewed on Milikia's face. "Okay, let's go already. Meet me at my camp." He climbed into his truck and tore down the road.

The captain was waiting for them, sitting at a card table playing solitaire.

Barry was standing beside him holding a scraggly, injured cat.

"We want you to go in and pretend you want to buy some guns. Take a good look around and report back to us. We just want to know what's going on in there."

"No problem."

They fitted him with a miniature camera and bugging device.

The captain scratched Barry's cat behind the ear. "If that thing pisses on my bed, you'll be cleaning it up."

Barry put the kitty in his comfy little box and pulled a milk carton from his pack.

The boys watched from the other side of the river.

Milikia drove into the yard, disappeared behind the bushes, climb out of the truck and cautiously made his way to the door. A body flew from behind a stack of bushes and shoved a gun into his face.

"I'm unarmed." He put his hands in the air.

"Who are you?"

Milikia pulled out his identification. "I was told by someone in the village that I may be able to purchase guns here."

The larger than life human eyed him up and down, then frisked him. "Who is this person in the village?"

"I don't remember his name. He was old and drunk and told me to come here."

"And what do you want the guns for?"

"What do you think?" He rolled his eyes.

The guy smiled. "Okay, come with me. Walk in front."

They entered the vast door, probably a servant's entrance at one time. Now a doorway to Satan. "Who lives here?"

"You don't know? This is the new headquarters for the Serbian underground militia. They bombed the other one. How many guns do you need?" They walked down a long hallway, then stairs that descended into a dark basement. He could hear women's voices off in the distance.

Milikia cringed.

They entered a large room. He was shocked. There was arsenal of all types, literally hundreds of guns. Four scruffy men sat in a corner playing cards and smoking raunchy cigarettes. The man from the front door told them why Milikia was there.

They quizzed him about where he lived and what he did. They showed him the arsenal, and made purchasing arrangements.

From the window above, Julie watched the cars and trucks come and go across the bridge. She wished so much for Nick to find her. She wished he would come and set her free. She fantasized the fairy princess story where her knight in shining armor rescued her.

As quickly as her fantasy started, it ended. She snapped out of her daydream and back into reality.

"We need to get bugs in there. Can you befriend them somehow and possibly plant some?" the captain asked.

Milikia thought for a minute. "Cards. They were playing cards, maybe I could talk them into a card game."

"Might work. Let's give it a try."

"It's all set up. Big poker game this Saturday night," Milika told the captain, a gleam in his eye.

The captain smiled. He gently pinched his cheek. "How'd you do that, my good friend?"

"It was my nephews. When we went in to get the guns, one of them knew one of them and just started talking about cards."

"Great. I'm going to give you these bugs." He showed him a variety of objects. "Leave them everywhere. Cigarette packages, pens, put this wad of gum in your mouth and stick it under the table or chair when you get in. Whatever you do, don't chomp on it, it has a mike in it." He showed him several other interesting devices.

Milikias eyes widened. He smiled and took the objects. "Do you think it's safe? What if they find them?"

"Can you get some more guys to go with you? Then they won't know who to expect."

Milikia thought for a minute. Maybe, maybe he could.

"We'll get Bessie to bake you a box of treats. We'll plant a bug in the box. Any other ideas?"

"No, I'm just a farmer. You're the spy pro."

"Okay then, keep in touch."

Without speaking and deep in thought, he turned and walked toward his truck.

"So you'll be in contact on Friday night?" the captain shouted after him. He so wanted to charge into the castle with all out force and guns blazing. Everyone knew it was better to move slowly, cautiously. Stake it out first.

Without looking back, Milikia waved his arm into the air, jumped in to his vehicle and drove away thinking about Saturday night.

The pub was empty, but quickly filled once the sun sat. He watched it go down from his seat by the window. A big red ball sinking into the earth. It didn't take him long to find five guys to help him play poker on Saturday night.

Chapter Twenty-Three

Nick sat at his laptop and stared at the empty screen. The cursor was blinking. His mind was a void. He couldn't stop thinking about Julie, wondering if the captain had followed up on Sam's vision. The phone rang. It was the captain. He chuckled at his own little bit of psychic power.

"We wanted to let you know that your friend was right on cue about that place. We haven't found Julie or the kid, but she definitely described the place to the *T.* There's some activity going on there. We're putting in bugs on Saturday."

"Bugs! Saturday! Today is Monday. You aren't going to search the place for her?"

"Too risky. Sorry. We wish we could, we hope she's safe, but Nick, think about it. It's the big guy we're after." His heartfelt sympathy was with the girls and millions of others just like them all over the world that life had dealt an unfair hand. The injustice was unthinkable.

Nick spun around. He couldn't wait until the weekend. He had to get back home. He had a story to write and couldn't wait any longer. "Put me on the next flight home, please."

"There's one going from the sea carrier tonight. I have two boys going home on it. I can't guarantee you a seat, but there are lots of ropes and straps to tie yourself down with."

"And the next civilian flight?"

"Won't be for a while. Maybe when the bombs have stopped."

"That's a long way without a seat. Okay, I'll take it."

"Bring a pillow. I'll send a truck to get you at five. Be ready to go at four."

Nick glanced at his watch. "That's in two hours."

"Very good."

"Thanks. And about Julie…"

"I'll call, I promise. I have your number right here. It's not something we're going to lose. We'll need you at The Hague someday. You're a witness."

"Thank you, Captain Smith, for everything."

"It's been my pleasure to work with you. And good luck with the story."

Nick was ecstatic. He hoped they were safe. He was torn. He wanted to wait to find Julie, but he wanted to go home and write his story. He started to pack his bag. Peace. World Peace. Total global world peace everywhere. It could be achieved. He knew it could be achieved. Somehow there had to be a way that human rights came first all over the world. That human rights come before government and religion and any other greed or hated belief.

He thought about his own Irish descent and wished someone in Ireland could achieve peace. Maybe it would send a shock wave around the world. If a cute, scenic little island full of hatred could learn peace, then maybe that would be the model. Ireland was a beautiful place, it could be rich from tourism, and instead they bred violence. And for what reason? If you ask ten Irish people what they fight about, you would get ten different answers. Religion, land, controls, but who cares. What matter was it had to end. It must be awful to think you need a terrorist group to protect you in your own country. Protect you from what? The ideology that one man's terrorist group is another man's freedom fighter? An ancient belief of people, who can't seem to get a life, cling on to like it's their inborn given right to hate and kill. Catholics and Protestants killing each other. Two religious groups not getting along. Two groups who claim to pray to the same God, hating each other. Some people would say that the British troops wouldn't leave Northern Ireland, but every time the North votes whether to stay under British rule or not, they vote to stay. The entire situation didn't make any sense.

Jack was waiting for him to write some big Kosovo story. His mortgage was overdue. Oh yeah, he had lottery money. He kept forgetting about the money. But the story. He felt like an unknown force was powering him. Someone was whispering in his ear to write about peace. But what about Julie? How long could he wait to see if she was okay? He needed to go home so he could start writing.

Nick sat down and wrote Julie a nice letter. The world flowed easily. He was surprised as his ability to express his thoughts to her so deeply and sincerely. He shoved it in an envelope and put it in her top dresser drawer.

He went out on to the back deck and looked out into the woods. Memories of the last few weeks flew through his mind. The sunrise, the angels, the doves, the kids playing war, Julie, the kid and of course, his story. His mind was in a thousand different places.

He took his last roach and burned his finger smoking it. Once the high hit, the creative juices began to flow. He could see the story materializing in his mind. It was like a statue beginning to form. The edges rough but soon to be crafted into something beautiful.

He locked up the house, put the key in the hiding spot, lugged his heavy pack outside, and sat on the curb. He stared at the house that had been hit with a rocket. It now lay flattened and in ruins.

The boys pulled up in a Jeep.

Nick was amazed as he checked his watch. It was exactly four.

"Are you Nick Saunders?" one of them yelled.

Nicked showed him his identification. The private glanced at it quickly. Nick opened the door and jumped in.

"Can't wait to get home," one of the said, "to that warm bed."

"I'm going to get my women," the other passenger mentioned.

Nick laughed. He thought about Samantha. A good romp in the sack with her would feel really good right now.

The two-hundred-kilometer ride to the coast took forever. Nick's hemorrhoids flared up. His voice went. The company was good. His

ELIZABETH MOULT

appreciation for the military continued to grow. What they went through in the name of peace.

The boys were both going home on compassionate leave. Scott's father had passed away, his mother was alone. Ian's son had been diagnosed with cancer.

The drive was beautiful, a thirty-eight-hundred mile coastline with seven-hundred and twenty-five islands. The Maritimes were so full of sun-baked villages and lots of wine. Buildings dating back to the seventeenth and eighteenth century. There was an excellent ferry service with one-hundred twenty ports of call. They boarded the ferry for the long ride to Italy.

Nick was wishing he could spend a few days there, but it wasn't going to happen. All he saw was the dock and a tarmac.

A chopper was waiting for them.

"Get ready to puke," Scott said. He and Ian laughed.

Nick gave them a bewildered look.

"Pilot said we're going to a restaurant before we head out."

Nick watched as the boys each gulped down three greasy hamburgers.

Ian burped eight times.

Nick looked out at the dark, choppy sea. "How far out to the carrier?"

"Long. Real long," Scott told him. The monotone in his voice and the look in his eyes indicated it was going to be a rough one.

"How do you know the captain?" Ian asked.

"I'm a witness."

"A witness. Don't tell us. Don't want to hear about it."

The boys weren't joking. The ride to the air carrier was long and bumpy. Nick was glad he hadn't eaten. He gave them a history lesson. "During the early seventeenth century there was a great migration of Europeans. Slavic tribes from the northeast began to colonize the Balkan Peninsula and area. Their descendants are the Slavic Nations that make up the former Yugoslavia. Many of the cities and roads in Yugoslavia are legacies of Greek colonization and Roman rule."

"All I know is I was sent to Kosovo with a gun on my back," Scott said.

Nick tried to sleep, but it was impossible. He closed his eyes and thought about Samantha. Then he thought about Julie and how guilty he felt leaving, but there was nothing he could do. He tried to blame himself because he didn't go with her that night, but deep down he knew he wasn't responsible.

By the time they reached the air carrier Nick was physically exhausted, but mentally wired.

"We can't fly right now," Scott told him after talking to someone who the traffic control people pushed out of the way. "There's a storm somewhere. They're going to give us a bed."

"Yahoo."

"You can leave your luggage in here." The young man pointed to a shed.

Nick watched as his friends threw their duffel bags in. He decided to lug his heavy pack the half-mile to the sleeping quarters. Nick was amazed at the size of the air carrier. It was the length of two and a half football fields. The tarmac was lined with Apache attack helicopters, B-52s, and F-16s.

They passed a group of women sitting in a lounge. One of them was putting on makeup.

Nick laughed and thought about the documentary where they said they didn't want women on board the air carriers because this wasn't a Carnival Cruise. She was an attractive woman. Nick wondered what she was doing in a place like this. It had to be the adventure. If she was doing her face, there was probably a man somewhere that she wanted to impress. Love knows no boundaries for the truly romantic.

He had the pleasure of meeting several people in the dining hall at breakfast. Their stories were full of compassion. They wanted to help innocent victims of corrupt politicians.

At exactly noon they heard their names over the loudspeaker to report to the tarmac, their Chinook was leaving at 12:00 hours. Don't be late.

Chapter Twenty-Four

Nick walked into his little empty house, thrilled to plunk his heavy pack on the couch. It was oh so good to be home. He didn't know what to do first. Should he phone Samantha? No, he should just leave her alone. He wasn't capable of the type of relationship she wanted, he was leading her on. She should get a life that didn't include him. He should phone Jack because he would be waiting for a story. He knew exactly what he was going to say.

"Nick. Where's my story?" Jack asked without inquiring about his well being.

Nick's instincts were right. "I haven't written it yet." He waited the anticipated response.

"What? Well, get to it. I need it yesterday."

"I want to do something different with it," he begged.

"Like what?" Jack was impatient.

"Like peace." His voice was somber. Again he knew what the response was going to be. He heard his squeaky chair spin. "Looking at the skyscraper?"

"Yes, we have to move. Anita is already doing a story on peace. What's with everyone wanting to write about something even the Catholic Pope can't achieve? I spent a lot of money sending you to Kosovo, Nick. You wanted to go there, now I want my story. And hurry, it's starting to be old news."

Nick knew there was no point in arguing with him, not if he wanted to keep his job. "Fine. I'll start this afternoon."

"You have forty-eight hours. Bring me the story and I'll put you back on the payroll. Oh, and by the way, welcome home." He hung up the phone.

Nick stood in his living room holding the receiver in his hand, staring at it and listening to the buzz of the dial tone. Finally he put it in the cradle and went next door to fetch Spud, his cat.

"He's been having a great time," Randy told him.

"Thanks, I owe you."

"It's no big deal. How was Kosovo?" his good friend asked.

"Interesting to say the least. One of the most interesting and bizarre experiences of my life."

"I saw Samantha a while ago. She's really hung up on you."

Nick knew that. He smiled but said nothing.

"Smoke?" He pulled his cigarettes out of his pocket.

"No thanks. I quit,"

"You quit. Wow, how'd you do that?"

He remembered grounding his last butt into a pulp in front of the camera store. "Don't know, just did."

Nick wrote Jack's story. And as he'd told himself over and over, it was bullshit. It was people killing people because of religion or whatever. It had been going on forever. There'd been so many wars fought in the name of religion. That must really impress God.

"What's wrong with you?" Jack asked as he flipped through the manuscript. "This is the worst crap you've ever written."

His response didn't surprise him. It was something he'd hammered out quickly.

"It has no depth. You just touched the surface. Everyone knows it's about religion. I thought you were going to write about how it affects people's lives and all that stuff?" He was staring at him, his neck stuck out like a chicken waiting for the axe.

"I *told* you I wanted to turn it around and write about peace." He admired the new furnishings in the board room.

"And I told you that Anita was doing a story on peace. Now go back to your keyboard and give me something I can use. Please. You're turning into a pacifist."

Nick gave him the evil eye. "A what?"

"A pacifist. Oh, don't tell me you don't know what a pacifist is. It's someone who is in opposition to war and other violence. Absolute pacifists are against all wars and against violence in any form whatsoever."

"So what's wrong with that?"

"It doesn't sell, Nick. People want to read about people's hard luck. Unfortunately, that's what sells. Unless you're a Mennonite, of course."

He knew what he meant by that statement. Some religious groups such as the Mennonites believe they can convert aggressors to peaceful ways by setting an example of loving and nonviolent behavior. It was this attitude that was expressed in the New Testament Sermon on the Mount.

"Look at these pictures, Jack." Once again he shoved his pictures in his face.

"I've seen them already." He quickly looked through them. "Anyone can do this, Nick. The pictures are good, but anyone can do this."

"Do what?"

"Trick photography. And don't give me any crap about some angel you met."

Nick sat silent for what felt like an eternity. He looked at the lines on his face and decided they were permanently turned downward. He should smile more.

Jack sipped his coffee, gazing back at him. The silence was deafening. Nick was mad. Jack was mad. The two of them struggled to control their tempers. Finally Nick couldn't take it anymore and got up to leave.

"Tomorrow, Nick." I want a story by tomorrow. And it better be good." His phone rang.

Nick could hear the voice screaming on the other end. "We got them back! We got the Rivlon account back."

"See what old-fashioned begging can do?" Jack told the voice.

Nick threw his hands in the air and kept walking. He didn't know what he was going to do because he knew he wasn't capable of doing anything else right now. He decided after all to stop and see Samantha.

"Nick, you're back." She threw her arms around him, happy as usual to see him.

"Hi," he said, somberly and totally unemotional.

"Tell me about Kosovo. Did you find your friend?" She made him a cup of tea.

Nick proceeded to tell her about his trip and how he was having such a difficult time with the story.

"I had another vision," she started to tell him.

"About Julie?"

"No, it's a peace thing. I saw a kid school program in war torn countries everywhere teaching peace education."

Nick realized she was picking up on his same thoughts. He'd had the same vision while sitting on Julie's back deck. "The United Nations has been trying for years to do that."

"Well, don't you think it's time they made a financial commitment to it?"

She led him to the living room, and then, in her usual seductive manner, seduced him to the point of exhaustion.

"We've been doing this for four years now, Nick."

He knew what she was getting at. She wanted more than casual sex. She wanted a relationship.

"It's all I'm capable of." He knew the words would probably hurt.

"It's okay. I understand."

He wondered if she really did.

As he drove away, he felt empty inside. He had to quit using Sam for just the sex. She continued to let it happen, but it was tearing him up.

He decided to visit Anita.

"Nick, I'm so happy to see you. Glad you made it back home safely." She opened the door wide for him to come in.

"Thanks, Anita. It's good to be home. I came to see how your story on peace is going."

"Okay. I've been dealing with Amnesty International. They're an organization who accomplishes their goals through letter writing because, as Peter Gabriel would say, 'The written word is more powerful than the sword.'"

"That's it?"

"It's hard, Nick. It isn't an easy topic to cover. They love the coverage, it's like free advertising for them."

Nick wondered how Anita got free rein with Jack and he couldn't.

"What's going on with you?"

"I'm not sure. Jack didn't like my story."

"Well, I just saw it. Nick, it's not your usual stuff."

"I know. I have other things on my mind. There are so many organizations dealing with the peace issue and have been doing so for decades. It surprises me they haven't accomplished more than they have."

"I know, and another thing that surprises me is that so many of the humanitarian crises and violence are occurring in countries who are members of the United Nations. The main purpose for the development of the United Nations was for peace and the protection of human rights. They don't play by their own rules."

"They should impose an education tax on all members. A tax that goes to ensuring every child on the planet gets a school and lunch program. Set it up so that an entire generation of kids from around the globe are educated all at once and have it include a strong peace education program. The United Nations would be forced to deal with the poverty issue because they would be swimming right in it."

"That's a good idea, Nick. It would be a start anyway. The planet also needs to get a major grip on birth control."

"I know but in the meantime we have crisis that need to be dealt with."

He left Anita's, went to the ocean, and watched the waves crash into shore then roll back out to sea, churning ideas in his brain. He decided he would have to write a novel. There was no other way. He would write a novel about how world peace could be achieved. Suddenly it all came together in his mind.

"Where's Nick? Anita asked Jack.
"Off on leave again. He's in some kind of state about something that happened to him in Kosovo. I can't figure him out. He's into a world peace thing. Don't ask me," Jack said. He was mad. Nick had never redone the Kosovo story. Jack ended up using the one he'd previously written, buried it in the back of the magazine. It had cost a ton of money to set Nick up over there. He'd expected something better. It wasn't like Nick. Jack simply wrote it off as burnout. One simple reporting tour to a corrupt country can do that to one. It's happened before and will happen again. You don't come back the same person. It can change your life and outlook on things forever.

Chapter Twenty-Five

Milikia showed up at the door with seven other guys and an old basket of muffins from Bessie. "Mom sent treats. I hope you don't mind that I brought along a few friends. They're all Serbs."

The guy at the door clung tight to his gun. "Your mom sent treats?" He emptied the basket out on the stone wall then checked their papers. "How much money you got? We play for big."

Everyone pulled out a big wad of cash the captain had given them.

"I guess it'll be okay. Come with me."

As they walked down the hallway they could hear women screaming from down the hall. "Over here. Help us please, we're over here." Milikia wanted to shove the guy and run to them. He refrained.

"We have some extra curricular activities down there if anyone gets in the mood."

Milikia felt sick. He knew what that meant. They had women locked up and were using them for sex. He wondered how people could succumb to such activities. "Maybe later. We're here to play cards."

"Oh, you guys are serious card players." He flashed a big grin. "One-hundred dinars stake."

They had no problems planting the bugging devices. They won money, lost it, and won it all back. As night progressed into dawn, everyone was totally inebriated.

Upstairs, Julie and Alexis sat at their little table playing cards.

"Are we ever going to get out of here?" the freckled face child asked.

Julie smiled tenderly. "Yes, we will. I'm sure of it."

She thought of Nick and wondered what had happened to him. More than anything she wondered what it was like to live in a world where there was no war, no hate, and no killing. It would be wonderful if everyone could have a sane, democratic government. Politicians who honestly care for the well being of all the people, no discrimination because of their religion, ethnic values or border.

A few days later, the captain visited Milikia. "I want you to know that the bugs have been very useful. We've been able to track their activities. We're setting up a raid. We are going to go in, confiscate the guns and free the women."

Milikia hugged him so hard that he almost knocked the wind out of him.

The Captain returned to the barracks and wrote a letter of appreciation to the psychic named Samantha whose vision will help to free the girls.

Chapter Twenty-Six

Samantha read the thank you card from the Captain. She smiled and placed it carefully on the mantle. It had a foot and mouth painting on it. A pretty landscape scene of soft rolling hills with wildflowers.

The doorbell rang.

She opened the door to find the neighborhood kids smiling up at her, their faces smeared with purple goop.

"Did you know that you have berries?"

Sam thought about the berry crumb cake she was planning to bake. She smiled tenderly at their innocent, playful faces. "Are they good?"

"Yup, yummy. What are you doing?" the little blonde girl asked.

"Working on my novel. What are you doing?"

"Swimming in the river."

She noticed their wet hair.

"Do you want to go for a bike ride?"

The wind blew their hair as they rode the scenic, peaceful river trail.

Samantha called the river park a little piece of Heaven because that's what it was, a little piece of Heaven. They were free and happy. Nothing was better for the soul than the sound of childrens laughter.

They rode into the sunset. The sky turned five brilliant colors. At the bend in the river there was a beautiful rainbow. They peddled home in the twilight. She thought about her simple, uncomplicated life. She was proud to be Canadian and felt fortunate to be living under a sane government.

She thought about Nick and prayed for his safety.

Later that night, she sat dreaming out the kitchen window and thinking about how God had sent Jesus to teach us how to love one another and help the less fortunate.

When she slept, she had a dream about a child angel. A golden statue of a small boy with wings. It'd taken life and flown around the room, a strange light radiating from it. It fluttered about a few times then settled back into its frozen statue.

She'd purposely woken herself up. Had it been a dream or just another vision? She couldn't figure out what it meant. The light on the bedside table flickered and then went out. It was probably the fuse box. She needed a new one, but there was no money for stuff like that.

She'd probably just keep changing fuses forever.

Chapter Twenty-Seven

It was a dark, cloudy, rainy day. Lightning flashed in the sky. A bang of thunder roared.

Nick sat down at his keyboard and wondered why he hadn't thought of it before. A novel. The words flowed easily. It would be a story about a reporter who wrote a novel about how world peace could be achieved. He thought about Julie and Alexis. It was for them and the millions of others who constantly live in a world of corruption and hate that inspired every word. It was thoughts of them that motivated his actions to write with such depth, emotion, and determination. Maybe this was what the angel had meant by saying they could help. It was as though the rest of the world didn't exist. It was just he and his little keyboard of letters. When he researched world peace, he was surprised at what he found. The number of organizations that were involved in peace was phenomenal. There was the United Nation's education, scientific, and cultural organizations. One of their main priorities was establishing a culture of peace through education. And UNICEF, an organization that focused on long term human developing countries. He was surprised to learn they were an agency of the United Nations. And the Peace Corps, a U.S. agency that was created to promote world peace and friendship by training American volunteers to perform social and humanitarian services overseas. The Ford Foundation, who among other things was concerned with human rights, arms control, international peace and security. The Freemasons were concerned with peace. The American Veterans Committee, they too worked internationally to promote peace. And then there was the Organization of American States; again one of their main purposes is to strengthen the peace and security of the continent.

He took a break and made a cup of coffee. It was mind-boggling. As he watched the brown water bubble in the microwave, so many thoughts came to him about these organizations. There were so many of them, and still so much violence in the world.

As he sipped the hot steamy liquid, he continued his research. There was the World Council of Churches, where peace was one of the major subdivisions.

The Young Women's Christian Association, one of their goals is to attain peace, justice, freedom and dignity for all people. The Writers for Peace Committee, which was a subcommittee of International PEN and based in Slovenia. They explored ways in which writers could further the cause of world peace. He would be sure to join.

There was the Carnegie Endowment for International Peace. A private foundation established in 1910 by philanthropist Andrew Carnegie for the purpose of abolishing war.

There were all of the organizations that dealt with the aftermath of war, like the International Court of Justice of the United Nations, more commonly known as The Hague, also known as the World Court, where the war crimes trials occurs that tries persons charged with criminal violations of the laws and customs of war and related principles of international law. And there was the Permanent Court of International Justice who facilitated the arbitration of international disputes. Of course, Amnesty International, who deals with prisoners.

He was happy to find the Presidential Medal of Freedom, an award that is presented annually by the President of the United States for outstanding contribution to security or national interest of the U.S. or world peace.

The Universal Declaration of Human rights was adopted by the United Nations General Assembly in 1948. It was a thirty-article declaration on human rights. That was a long time ago.

The oldest know treaty preserved in an inscription on a stone monument is a peace treaty.

He thought about Sir Winston Churchill's famous words, "Let there be justice for all."

"Nick."

He thought he heard someone say his name.

"Nick."

He heard the voice again. He spun around in his chair. No one is there.

"It's God."

Nick felt his eye widen. His body melted.

"I'm glad you asked for help with world peace. Not many people do that."

"What. Oh yeah. Yeah. I want to do that. I want to help. Are you really God?"

"Yes, Nick, but if you don't believe me, and a lot of people don't, then I'll just tell you I'm an angel. How's that?"

"Huh. Yeah. Okay." Nick was stunned. He pinched himself. He thought it was George Burns.

"I'm real. Don't worry."

"Nick, you need to deal with the politicians. It's the politicians you need to deal with, because they are the ones who are responsible for their people. Good leadership starts with a good leader. I too am sick of the violence on the planet."

Lightning flashed in the sky. Then a bolt of thunder crashed so loud it hurt Nick's ears.

Nick jumped. "You. Did you do that?" He pointed out the window.

"I'm not responsible for stuff like that. I don't control stuff like that."

"Oh right. Okay."

"I gave you a spot in Raptures."

"In what? Raptures? What's that?"

"Look it up on the Internet."

Nick smiled. He was just like a normal human, only you couldn't see him.

"Basically, it is a group of people that I'm sparing for when the world ends and we start over. I'm picking a few hundred thousand people for that."

"What! You threaten people with the end of the world? What kind of a motivator is that? Instead of working toward the better of mankind, you threaten us with that? What kind of leadership is that?"

God chuckled. "I never met anyone like you before, Nick. I'm saving you a spot anyway. Nick…"

"Yes?"

"Why do you smoke pot?"

"Hey. Oh, I don't know. It stimulates my brain to be creative."

"Oh, is that why?" He chuckled. "I guess there's a lot I don't know."

Even God laughs. "I don't recommend it."

"I know, I invented it."

"Oh yeah, you did." Nick wondered why he did that. He began to ask, but God cut him off…

"Oh, and Nick…"

"Yes."

"I want you to use the Internet to help with the World Peace thing."

"You do. Oh, okay."

"I can't use it."

Wow, so he wasn't technologically wired.

"Good luck, Nick. I'm leaving now. I'm very busy and won't be back for a while, but I'll continue to send messengers."

"Thanks. Yeah. Thanks for the visit. It's been nice." Nick felt a presence exit the room. A cool breeze turned warm. He was stunned, but quickly hit the cursor for the Internet. After logging on, he keyed in "Raptures." He was sure it was a football team.

A list of web pages came up. Signs to look for. Books about the end of the world. Stuff about the Book of Revelations, the return of Christ. It was baffling. He didn't believe half of it, in fact, he believed very little of what is written in the Holy Scriptures. The way he saw it was, that God had sent Jesus to teach us how to love one another and help the less fortunate. Here it was almost two-thousand years since then and not much had changed. He also didn't believe that Jesus died for our sins. Pontius Pilate murdered him. And Mary thought she'd never see his face again. So many demons had probably played with the Holy Bible over the years that it probably wasn't worth worrying about. He'd never read it because he thought it contained too much violence. Nick honestly believed that man could save the planet if he really wanted to. The politicians really do set the pace for the way a country contributes to the over all well being of the globe. Each politician does his little part to a larger scale of global commitment. Commitment to stopping wars so that every human can live a fair and happy existence. A commitment to creating sustainable environments, getting a grip on world population explosion and riding the world of evil. Evil had lurked in the shadows of corrupt countries for too long. It was time they were gone. Bye, bye. Time to go. A new breed of leadership is needed for this planet that is so filled with hate for one another that they kill for stupid reasons. This would be a new start for earth.

Nick began typing. He created a character similar to him, only different, who would set the stage for a global transformation that would rid the world of evil and unfairness. There would be justice for all.

He went for a hike in the park, returned, and made a cup of tea. He sat down to check his e-mails.

"Tell them to get rid of the crucifix. Jesus is sick of it. He wants to be remembered by how he lived not by how he died."

Nick twirled around. No one was in the room.

"Yes, and tell them that Mary Magdalene wasn't a prostitute. She was very much in love with Jesus. They were a couple."

Nick felt his eyes widen.

"And tell them not to pass same sex marriage. Tell them not to do it."

"Huhhhhh?"

"And God wants the planet to write a new set of Holy Scriptures. One that tells the truth about everything. One that will guide the planet into creating a fairer and more sustainable world."

"Who are you?"

"God is getting mad."

"About what?"

"All the crap going on. Man is destroying himself."

"No joke. It's been happening for years. Who are you?"

"Oh, just someone. Just do it. I have to go."

"Wait."

No one answered.

Nick wondered if he needed pharmaceutical drugs. He knew what he heard. Now he just wondered what to do with the information. He felt like he should tell the Pope or something. It sounded important.

Nick keyed in the last word to his novel and hit the period button. He inserted a disc, copied the last chapter and then made three copies. This was one piece of work he didn't want to lose.

He sat back in his chair and admired his computer. He was proud of his accomplishment and wanted his own private celebration. He walked over to the wine cabinet and took a bottle of red wine that a friend had given him over five years ago. It would be well flavored by now. Carefully he removed the cork and smelled the aroma. The scent was inviting. He put the bottle down to breath and checked his messages Samantha had called again for the fifth day in a row. He returned her call.

"Can you come over?"

"You can't let go, can you?"

There was a long silence. "Guess not."

"I can't come over now. I'm tired and busy."

"Okay. I'll try you again sometime."

"You should just give up on me. I'll never be capable of anything more than a casual relationship."

They said goodbye.

The phone rang. He checked the call display, it was long distance, and he didn't recognize the number.

"I need you to come to Kosovo with me, Nick," the captain said. "The United Nations wants me to videotape you at the site with you describing what you saw. This is important, Nick. We need you to do this."

179

Nick contemplated the captain's words. The nightmares about that day were finally beginning to stop. He was wishing he would never have to deal with it ever again.

"When?"

The captain gave him the details.

"What about Julie? Did you ever find her?"

"We raided the house and set free about twelve women who'd been used for months as sex slaves. There was no sign of your friend. She'd been there because the girls remember her, but she wasn't around. We found a mountain of arsenal and explosives though. It was a good tip from that friend of yours."

"Yes. She does have her moments."

"Sorry. I know that's not what you want to hear."

Nick said a silent prayer for her and Alexis. He knew in his heart that she was still alive and still needed help.

As Nick suspected, returning to the site was difficult. He was expecting to bump into his angel. He hadn't seen her since the kids were playing war out back. She wasn't around.

Nick barely recognized the place. The site was overgrown with weeds. Most of the surviving villagers had left. Memories tore into him like a dagger. It was extremely painful to think back. He looked off into the direction of the field he'd spent that insane night. He thought about the sky, the doves, the angels, the harps, and the voices. Maybe he'd imagined everything. After all, he had been in shock. If it hadn't been for his pictures he would really be questioning his own sanity.

"Can we go to the place where Julie was?" Nick asked after the interview was over.

The captain looked at him. "The guerillas are still using the place as their headquarters. They moved back in about a week after the raid. The bugs are still in place. We're still monitoring it. The United Nations has left a ton of peacekeepers here and we think they'll probably stay for at least a decade so things don't flare up again. We can go look, Nick, but I have to tell you. We've had that place bugged for many months now. There hasn't been any mention of her."

Nick could see the castle from the other side of the river. It was an eerie place with vines growing everywhere. They crossed the bridge and drove to the door.

"Are you just going to knock on the door?" Nick wondered.

"Oh, they know me. They know if they don't let us in, I'll be back with force."

The interpreter described Julie and the little girl to the moron at the door.

"No. Haven't seen anyone like that around."

Nick could tell he was lying.

"We're going in," the captain said. He signaled to the Jeep full of soldiers who jumped into action. They barged past the big tough dumb guard with the tattoo on his arm that said, "Mom." The guy was actually human.

They searched the entire place. There was a big card game happening. The smoke was so thick you couldn't see across the room. There was no sign of Julie and the girl.

They returned to their vehicle, climbed in and drove across the bridge and along the river road. Nick glanced up toward the upper windows. "Stop," he shouted. "Quick. Give me those binoculars."

Nick jumped out of the Jeep and looked up to the top window of the large building. Then he saw them. He wasn't absolutely positive, but it definitely resembled them. He vaguely made out the two figures in the window. He was sure they were Julie and Alexis.

Chapter Twenty-Eight

"Parafont pictures wants to buy your novel," the voice over the phone told Samantha.

She looked at the pails under the leaky roof, it would soon be overflowing if she didn't empty it. "They what!" she screamed, not believing what she'd just heard.

"Parafont pictures want your novel. The one about the Colombian drug war. I hope you don't mind that I shopped it in Hollywood. In all honesty, Samantha, I think it would make a better movie than a book. Sorry."

Sorry. He was sorry. He shouldn't be sorry. "Don't be sorry. This is amazing news. This isn't a joke, right? You aren't pulling my leg or anything?"

"Not at all. I'll send you the contract in the mail. Fifty-thousand for the rights to the book and two percent of all movie profits. It's a good story; it reaches into the reality of the peasants."

"Wow. Thank you." She was glad she'd found an agent who was willing to work for free on her behalf until something sold. She didn't know if fifty-thousand was a good sum of money for something like that, but one thing she did know was that it would fix her leaky roof. She couldn't wait to tell Nick because she was sure he thought she wouldn't accomplish anything. He'd been wrong.

The doorbell rang. There was a man standing there with flowers. "Awe, Nick came to his senses." She thanked the deliveryman and set them on the table. A warmth filled her heart. She saw a possible future with Nick. After admiring them carefully, she slowly opened the card and gasped at the signature. They were from Julie and Alexis. The card read:

"Dear Samantha, words cannot express the appreciation we have toward you for sharing your psychic vision with Nick. I was told that it was your vision that helped to find us. Thank you again. Sincerely, Julie and Alexis."

Samantha sat down and cried bittersweet tears.

For some unknown reason Nick's words, "you never give up," echoed in her mind over and over like a broken record stuck on an irritating tune. She looked out the window and said, "Yes, Nick. I just did."

Chapter Twenty-Nine

Mrs. Peterson gazed out the window as she washed the dishes. She could see the mailman coming up the sidewalk as he always did every day at this time. She finished the last dish and pulled the plug. The grief she'd endured this past year over the loss of her son Jeff had been unbearable. She was beginning to feel a bit better.

She opened the door and reached into the mailbox, flipped through the usual flyers and bills. There was a letter postmarked New Jersey. She recognized the name. It was Jeff's old army friend, Rob. Quickly she ripped open the letter and was surprised to find a picture of a girl holding a small baby. She didn't understand. She read the letter.

Dear Mr. Peterson:

Please do not be shocked by what I'm going to tell you. It is not uncommon for something like this to happen in the military. This is your grandchild. He was conceived the day Jeff was shot. The mother, Nadine, wanted to let you know that you have a grandchild and to say hello. The child's name is Jeffery Robert.

She wanted you to know that she knew nothing about the setup when Jeff was killed. The men gave her money to distract them. She said she'd fallen in love with your son at first sight.

We found the person who shot Jeff. Nadine is willing to testify on Jeff's behalf. Your son's killer will be brought to justice.
If you need any more answers, please call me.

Love to all,
Rob.

The words were comforting in her world of pain and grief. She gazed into the eyes of the child and could see her son looking up at her. She was overcome with joy and happiness. Immediately she put the wheels in motion for the young girl and the baby to come live with them.

She had many unanswered questions about Jeff's death, but the only thing that mattered right now was to help raise his child.

Julie opened her office door. She was now a nurse at a sexual assault center in Canada. Alexis lived with her. The girl sitting on the bed was curled up, crying and tightly holding her legs together. Julie's experiences from the war in Kosovo had made her one of the best sexual assault counselors who'd ever worked at the clinic. She thought back to the day when Nick and fifty peacekeepers had rescued her from the castle where she and Alexis had been held for so long. They'd missed their room during the first raid because the door, the one beside the golden statue of the boy angel, was hidden in a wall. They'd had it good there in comparison to others. They'd simply been lucky. Still, the memories were there, the nightmares never went away, but life went on. She was grateful to be alive. She was grateful to Nick for helping her. She wished he'd wanted a relationship with her, but he claimed to like his freedom too much. She thought back to the letter she'd found in her dresser drawer from him, apologizing for leaving them when he wasn't sure of their whereabouts or safety. He was grateful for the friendship during a difficult and confusing time. He'd apologized for his sexual inadequacies and explained he just wasn't capable of a relationship with anyone, he was too absorbed in his work.

Jack summoned Anita into his office. "I've decided to give you your own weekly column entitled 'Peace Education.'"

Anita smiled and hugged her boss. He'd finally seen the light. "I feel the media has a responsibility to bring the success stories to light as much as the hard luck ones."

"The planet is changing, as Nick would say. Tyrant governments simply have to go."

Chapter Thirty

"I think it has the qualities of a best seller," the publisher was telling Nick.

His eyes grew. It hadn't been his intention to write a best seller, it was his intention to write something that would help world peace.

"I'll have the contract drafted up. Take some time with it. You may want to take it to your agent or the writer's union."

Nick was stunned. He didn't have an agent. He didn't belong to the writer's union. "And your pictures, the ones with the angels that you claim to be authentic." He sounded apprehensive. "We put them into one large coffee table book. They're really sensational. Do you have a name in mind? For the larger picture book?"

Nick thought for a moment. "The Face of Peace? The goal is to create awareness in people."

"The goal is to create an awareness in people."

He decided to visit Samantha, hoping she'd help him celebrate. Instead she introduced her new lover to him.

"But you said you'd love me forever."

"Doesn't mean we should live together."

She had a point.

"And I sold one of my novels to Parafont pictures," she told him.

Nick walked away breathless. She'd finally done it. She'd finally given up on him. She'd actually sold one of her novels. He couldn't believe it, especially the part about the new lover. It made him sad. Suddenly he wanted and needed her now more than ever, but it was too late. He'd been so busy and involved in his quest to better the world that he'd forgotten to take care of another important matter, his own need for companionship. He'd no one to blame but himself.

He went to visit Julie.

She and Alexis welcomed him with open arms.

Three weeks later the phone rang. "Nick, you've been nominated for the Nobel Peace Prize for your novel *Doves and Angels*," Jack, his newly appointed agent, told him. "Congratulations, Nick. I read it, it's quite the concept. The United Nations wants you to go to their next pow-wow and explain the theory behind it. They want to hear about the concept from you in person."

Nick was flattered He would love to go. He was on a quest for peace in a troubled world.

"Also, they want to enlarge the pictures from your book, *The Face of Peace* and build a special Peace museum to display them. The goal is to create awareness in people of the need to end war."

"Yes, the first step to solving the poverty issues is to end the wars and the violence. It's costing the planet billions. Money that could be so better used."

Nick gazed out at the General Assembly. The auditorium was packed. He'd insisted they charge a small admission fee to listen to him speak. The proceeds would go to the child education fund. No child on the planet gets left behind.

"The concept is basically this: Mankind has a responsibility to create peace and sustainability. This is one planet that we all share. As we must start listening to the scientists who tell us we have a serious global warming problem and who been warning us about it for decades, we also have a serious hatred problem. The earth has many problems. It is the leader of individual countries who are responsible to help solve the problems. Everyone works toward a common goal: saving planet earth from global destruction and creating a fairer planet for all. And that includes getting a grip on population explosion.

All the different religious leaders should join together to create a New World Law. Human Rights come first above and over everything else. No government on planet earth has the right to violate the International Charter of Human Rights. There will be a new set of world rules for the United Nations. It will include a law that states that people who lead countries as government will be subjected to a mental sanity test developed by psychologists from around the globe, a test to determine if the individual leader is 'sane' enough to be running a country.

All the peace organizations join together to form the most powerful organization on the face of the earth with a new Universal Declaration of Human rights. Membership is mandatory; every country in the world must join. It's a mandatory objective of the Universal Human Rights.

There's a mandatory child education taxation fee. No child left behind. Every child on the planet goes to school.

There are so many organizations that work independently of each other and if they all joined to form one union, they would be more powerful. I wonder how many peace organizations there are in Kosovo. They could form a union and sell cheap memberships similar to the writer's union, simply a voice that keeps everything under control.

The reporter in my novel took a worldwide vote from all heads of state around the world and majority rules. This is now to be the law of the land. Peace education must be taught in every school setting on the planet, from the toddler to the university folks.

Heads of State who allow atrocities to occur on their land will be sentenced under the New World Peace Act. The planet creates a mandatory program on world peace and respect for human rights.

Peace and human rights are the ultimate goals and there will be zero tolerance."

He looked out at the vast audience. Never in his wildest dream did he ever believe he would come this far in one year.

The outside courtyard was full of people. Nick stood proud on the platform.

"And the recipient for the Nobel Peace prize goes to Nick Sanders for his two books, *Doves and Angels,* and *The Face of Peace.*"

He'd insisted that the only medal they give him was one that he could hang around his neck. In the courtyard they did just that. At that very moment the entire sky around the world turned the most incredible color of red, orange and yellow.

Then, and almost as though he expected to see her there, she appeared. His angel. Floating above.

The entire audience gasped in awe. There was silence of the most penetrating kind. The beautiful vision opened her wings and spoke, "I come before you today on God's behalf. Peace must start in the heart of the individual. He wants two things: First, that the religious leaders of the world form a New World Religion. One that is fair, respects the individual, acknowledges that Jesus didn't die for our sins, but was murdered and prepares the planet for the next Messiah.

Also, he's requested the entire world must now join membership in the International World Peace Crown Committee. A committee of the Lord God. A committee that will ensure peace among all citizens. Membership is mandatory to every living citizen on this planet. The Lord, our God has spoken. Let this be your law."

Millions and millions of angels with harps started to play and sing the most sensational melody anyone had ever heard. Doves of an uncountable magnitude filled the skies all over the planet, each spreading its wings and flying in a most graceful glide. It was the most incredible sight anyone had ever seen in their entire lives. From that moment on, everyone knew there had to be peace on earth.

Nick looked out at the amazing view and knew he wasn't crazy after all. But darn, he didn't have his camera.

Nick set the medal on his coffee table and poured a glass of red wine. He felt like the Pope. He picked it up and looked at the peace dove engraving, feeling it with the tip of his finger, running it over the ruffled feathers.

"Congratulations Nick."

Nick looked around. There was no one.

"Your mother must be proud."

"She's dead."

"She's still proud."

"Who are you?"

"It's God. Don't you recognize my voice?"

"Oh yes. Okay. Yes, I remember you."

"Good."

"I have a mission for you. I want to send another son to earth. Prepare the world for me."

"What?"

"Do you have a woman somewhere?"

"Do you know Samantha Harrington?"

"Yes, I know Samantha. She'd be good."

"Well, she's with someone else now."

"Oh yes, right. That seems to be the trend these days. Tist, tist."

So he cared that the family was in fracture.

"So, do you want to do it?"

"Do what?"

"Be the father."

Nick was stunned. He couldn't believe what God was asking him to do, be the parent for the next Messiah. He thought about it for a few minutes. His health wasn't all that great. He didn't feel like he had the stamina for the demands of parenthood. "No thanks, I'm too old. I've abused my body with alcohol and smoke for years."

"I can fix that."

For about ten seconds Nick felt completely healthy and energized.

"That was just an example."

It was a tough decision. He'd have to join sainthood. He liked his private life. He really felt as though someone younger would be better. His life would take a dramatic turn and be put under a microscope. He was honored that God had considered him, but he enjoyed his writing career. Besides, look what they did to Jesus, no parent should have to endure that type of grief. The murder of Christ.

"I'd do it, except basically, he'd need protection. Look what they did to Jesus. Get Prince Harry."

"Prince Harry. Why him? *Oh yeah, Princess Diana...*" his voice trailed off.

"His mother was a humanitarian and he'd have protection with the British Army."

"Why not William?"

"He'll be too busy being King. Harry should just find a sweet, innocent little farm girl somewhere. And he'd need to have magical powers."

"Oh, he'll have *powers* alright. I want to send him to study with the Monks in India. That's what I did with the last one. They called him Isa."

He spoke as though *"the last one,"* was one of several. He wondered exactly how many sons he'd sent to earth over the years. "Highest elevation on earth. The closest to you. Why the monks?"

"Because they practice good fellowship."

"Why don't you send a daughter?"

"A daughter. Why a daughter?"

"I don't know, something different."

"Never thought of it."

"Why did you ask Abraham to sacrifice his son?"

"To prove that he was committed to me."

"That was an awful thing to do. What kind of God are you?"

"Even I am fallible. Even I make mistakes."

"And what about Jesus? How could you allow them to do that to him? And the Jews claim they were abandoned by God."

"I can't control people's behavior. That's why I send angels."

"You should get Mel Bibson to make a movie about what they did to Jesus."

"Why him?"

"I don't know. He likes to direct movies."

"He's already on to it."

Once again Nick was amazed at his own little psychic power. Maybe he read it in People magazine or something.

Nick thought he heard a faint voice speaking from behind God.

"I have to go," he told him. "I'll be back."

"Okay, Bye." Nick waved. He wondered who'd summoned him away. Probably the Pope.

The cool breeze left the room. A shiver went down his spine. What was he supposed to do with all that information? Tell someone at CNN?

That night Nick dreamt in technicolor. He saw three clouds hovering in the sky. One was of the Virgin Mary, one a baby in a basket, the third of Mother holding child. It had to be some kind of a sign. He wished he could take pictures of his dreams with his camera. He was passionate about his work.

Preclude

In September 2000, the United Nations set seven Major Millennium Development Goals. The Global Agenda for the twenty-first century to be accomplished by the year 2015.

All 191 United Nations Member states pledge to:

-Eradicate extreme poverty and hunger: Halve the proportion of people living on less than a dollar a day and who suffer from hunger.

-Achieve universal primary education: Ensure all boys and girls complete a full course of primary schooling.

-Promote gender equality and empower women: Eliminate disparity in primary and secondary education preferably by 2005, and at all levels by 2015.

-Reduce child mortality: Reduce by two thirds the mortality rate among children under five.

-Improve maternal health: Reduce by three-quarters the maternal mortality ratio.

-Combat HIV/Aids, malaria and other diseases: Halt and begin to reverse the spread of HIV/AIDS and the incidence of malaria and other major diseases.

DOVES AND ANGELS

-Ensure environmental sustainability: Integrate the principles of sustainable development into country policies and programs; reverse loss of environmental resources. Halve the proportion of people without sustainable access to safe drinking water and significantly improve the lives of at least one-hundred million slum dwellers by 2020.

On September 11/2001, fifteen men, ten whom were native to Saudi Arabia, high jacked and slammed two planes in the New York trade Center, a plane into the Pentagon, and one headed for the White House was overthrown by the passengers and crashed in a field.

Osama bin Laden sent videotape of him and his psychotic friends cheering the event. He claimed the prophet Muhammad had spoken to him in his sleep and told him to wage holy war with the West. It would be their key to Paradise. Muhammad is Allah's (God's) messenger. If that was true, Nick figured that Muhammad was now a fallen arch-angel or better known as Satan or the devil.

The Americans responded by bombing terrorist training camps in Afghanistan. They then invaded the Middle East in an effort to wipe out terrorism, starting with Saddam, the madman in Iraq, who'd played so many games with the weapons inspectors over the years. He had everyone believing he had weapons of mass destruction. No one trusted him.

The terrorist actions of September 11/2001, and pervious attacks, sparked a reign of terror that would eventually cost the planet billions of dollars on security. Money promised for the millennium goals now went to wiping out terror. Many people fear it is the start of World War III.

November 2001
Nick surveyed his cluttered office. Every day a new file or book was added. The room now looked like someone cleaned out a classroom.

The phone rang. He checked the call display. It was Samantha. He wondered what she wanted. Maybe she still loved him and was coming back. He quickly picked up the receiver. "Hi, Sam."

She wasn't coming back. She was happy with her new lover and was getting married. "They need to do something about Saddam."

"What?"

"I had a vision."

Nick grabbed his notebook. From now on he was going to listen to her when she told him stuff like that. "And…"

"And he's dangerous."

"And…"

"Well, it's not a clear vision but there's a major explosion and he's involved."

Nuclear weapon. Nick felt the blood sink to his feet.

He took a hike in the woods to absorb her thoughts. He was back home in Ontario and it felt great. He'd given up his job with the *Tribute* and was now freelancing. He hiked to the little spot where he prayed to God and thanked him for his wonderful life.

"Dear God, please help the President make the right decision about dealing with Iraq."

"Nick."

He heard a voice.

"God said to remind you that *he's* God."

"Okay, I'll shut up then."

He heard God's voice from above. "No, don't do that. I have something special planned for you."

"You do? Like what?"

"Pope on the new planet."

"What? Don't do that. They aren't allowed to have sex."

"I'm going to change all that."

"Get a woman to do it."

"That's a good idea. A female God for the new planet."

February 2002

Milosevic sat in court at The Hague faced with charges of war crimes.

He was accused of being the mastermind behind the murder of 900 Albanians and expulsion of 800,000 Kosovars from their homes. He also faced a trial of crimes against humanity and genocide in Croatia in 1991 and in Bosnia between 1992 and 1995. These included the expulsion of over 250,000 Croatian's and the massacre of over 7,000 Muslims in the town of Srebrenica in 1995.

September 2005

Seventeen-thousand and seventy-four Bosnian Serbs named as participants in the 1995 Srebrenica massacre of some 8,000 Muslim men and boys. It took eleven months after the Serb government acknowledged responsibility for the massacre before providing names.

Christmas 2005

Nick sat at his keyboard trying to decide what to write about next. He'd been researching Ireland and the IRA for years. But Ireland was now at peace and he felt his talents were needed elsewhere. He clicked on the Internet and played around with the mouse, checking out the sports page and who was doing whom in Hollywood. An instant message flashed on the screen. His gut instinct told him it was something interesting. He didn't recognize the name, but life is full of gambles.

It's a Bible thumper telling him to open his heart and get to know Jesus.

"I know the Father, but not the Son," he writes.

"Really?"

Nick didn't know if that was a question or not.

The guy gives him a prayer to say and then signs off.

Nick figured it was good advice anyway.

He went to his favorite place in the woods and prayed to God, telling him that he wanted to meet Jesus.

Several weeks passed.

Nick is in his kitchen trying to cook food that he almost always burns.

A voice sounded from across the room. "You said you wanted to meet me."

Nick was stunned as usual when stuff like that actually happens. "Ah, yes."

"And what was it that you wanted?"

Nick sensed Jesus wandering the room.

He admired a picture of himself with glowing halo and heart hanging on the wall.

Nick tells him someone sent it to him then asked for money. He'd hung it up anyway. "Someone said I should get to know you."

"Oh yeah." Jesus chuckled.

"I'm sorry, if I'd known you were coming I would have fixed things up a bit."

"That's okay. I can't stay long. Where's a good place to go?"

"For what?"

"Just to see."

Nick was baffled. Jesus wanted someplace to visit. "The beaches are nice."

"What beaches?"

"There's one in Prince Edward County and nice ones on Prince Edward Island."

"The names?"

"I don't know, someone just named nice places after Prince Edward."

"I know Prince Edward Island. What's the other one?"

"Prince Edward County. It's sort of one of the first islands of the start of the Thousands Islands down the St. Lawrence River."

"Ah."

"There's a big sand deposit that was left there after the last ice age."

"Oh I see. It's nice to learn new things."

Nick assumed he knew everything.

"What is it that you do?"

"Right now I'm reporting on political corruption and world peace."

"That's a big thing."

"I know."

"Where were you back then?"

"I'm sorry."

"You know my father, The God."

"I've spoken to him a couple times."

"He...he..." his voice trailed off.

Nick knew what he was trying to say. "They would have killed you anyway."

"They would have?" He sounded surprised.

"You represented everything they didn't want to change: fairness for all. Your Dad regrets what happened to you."

"He does?"

"Yes. I'm sure he does. You didn't die for everyone's sins, you were murdered."

"Oh I know, bunch of..." again his voice trailed off. "They drugged me up."

"I think it was one of the worst injustices ever. You weren't a criminal, you were God's son. And some where down the line..." Nick makes two finger quotation marks on each side of his head, "...'the died for our sins' part got added to the Bible. He wanted to maybe send another Messiah to earth, but we both said, 'look what they did to the last one.' I don't know what to say."

Nick sensed he felt angry and betrayed by both society and holy power. "Your father told me he can't control people's behavior. That's why he sends angels. I think it's the devil at work sometimes. I'm sorry about what happened to you."

"Ah, it's not your fault. Why did Mel Bibson make that movie about my crucifixion?"

"Probably to show the world what they did to you."

"Good."

"No mother should have to endure that type of grief."

"What about me?" His voice was filled with animosity.

Nick sensed he was tired of the injustice about what they'd done to his life. "That was horrific what they did to you."

"And they hang that thing of me everywhere..."

"I never did like that thing."

The room was silent, not the normal silence that happens from a lack of activity but a total dead silence.

"Can you ask Mel Bibson to make a movie to celebrate all the good that I tried to do."

"Sure. Where will he get his facts from?"

"I'll send messengers."

"Will do."

"Thanks. Well I guess we should be going."

"You don't want to stay for a while?"

He didn't answer for a few minutes. "Thanks for the visit."

"Before you go, can I say something?"

"Sure. What is it you want to say? You probably can't say anything that I haven't heard before." His voice sounded upset.

"I just want to apologize on behalf of mankind, if I may, not that my word means anything but, I just want to apologize for what they did to you."

"Thanks. Your word does mean something."

There was a peaceful type of silence in the room. Almost like time stood still.

"We'll we're leaving now. Thanks."

Before Nick had a chance to say anything, the room went calm. He felt their presence depart and wondered who it was that was with him.

February 2006

The Canadian Press reported: *Dozens See the Face of Jesus in a ʿince Edward Island Church.*

March 2006

Slobodan Milosevic dies of a heart attack in The Hague from possible self induced drug affliction. His crimes against him go unpunished.

The people of Yugoslavia are grateful to the NATO peacekeepers for removing him from power. Mass murderers should not be running countries.

October 2006

Nick goes for a hike in the municipal park to admire the fall leaves. The array of color and cool crisp air is refreshing after the long hot summer.

He stops at the war memorial that the local Legion maintains and reads the engraving on it.

In honored and lasting memory of our friends, relatives and neighbors who have made the ultimate sacrifice so we may continue to enjoy freedom, justice and liberty.

A beautiful white dove landed on top of the stone monument, looked at Nick, chirped a few times in a determined noise then flew above the trees and down the river to the waterfall.

Nick watched its graceful glide. Tears roll down his cheek.
There is still so much work to do before the world achieves total peace.